AF392625

Imperfect Match

K. KIMUYU

Copy editor: Eunniah Mbabazi
Proofreader: M. Ruiyot
Cover designer: Stephen Njogu
Illustrator: John Babu
Author's website: www.kisauti.com

Copies of this book are available at the Kenya National Library.
ISBN 978-9914-764-30-7
To purchase this book, write to
talk@kisauti.com

I see your ugliness
and I see your beauty
and I wonder how
the same thing can be both.
— Markus Zusack

From me to you, always.

CONTENTS

Her Obsession

Monday, 7th August 2023

Wanja

From the window, Wanja watches Miriam—the woman her husband has been cheating on her with, and grips the boning knife in her pocket tightly. She stands outside the store, pretending to window-shop, and watches Miriam pick a pink cotton dress and take it to the check-out counter and wonders if she will use it to seduce her husband later.

Miriam exits the boutique, and Wanja looks the other way. Dressed in a black hoodie, baggy blue denim jeans, and black sneakers, she blends in. With her average height, hood pulled low, mask, sunglasses and backpack, she resembles a boy—but she still takes her precautions. She waits until Miriam is 10 steps ahead before starting to follow her.

Wanja stops at a Cold Stone. She asks for the price of vanilla ice cream while listening to the tapping of Miriam's heels receding on the mall's tiled floor. From the corner of her eye, she watches Miriam take the escalator. Wanja thanks the Cold Stone attendant, and walks in her direction. Her sneakers, silent on the tiles.

She watches Miriam's trouser suit and ponytail disappear into the basement and quickens her pace. Miriam turns towards the parking lot, and Wanja follows, gripping the boning knife tightly in her pocket. The parking lot is eerily quiet, save for the click of Miriam's heels on the pavement.

Wanja had planned to use her boning knife to scare her, but as she walks behind her, a darker urge creeps in. Her hand twitches, eager to sink the knife deep into Miriam's neck.

She draws closer—so close she can smell the vanilla notes of Miriam's Carolina Herrera, Good Girl perfume. Wanja begins to raise the hand clutching the boning knife, but the sudden sound of a car entering the parking lot stops her. She turns and walks in the opposite direction, and leans against a parked Toyota Voxy as though waiting for someone.

Wanja loosens her grip on the knife, astonished with herself. She hears chatter, followed by the sound of a car door opening and closing. From the side mirror of the Toyota Voxy, she watches in disbelief as her husband's Range Rover drives out of Two Rivers mall's basement parking lot. Wanja grips the boning knife again, her nails digging into her palm— now certain she wants to put an end to it.

Jack

JACK SITS IN the waiting area of his therapist's office on the second floor of Warwick Centre in Gigiri at noon. He is uncomfortable on the seat. Is it his charcoal gray suit? He unbuttons his coat, revealing a cream shirt, but it doesn't help. He picks up an old magazine on the coffee table as the soles of his black leather shoes tap the floor softly. He begins flipping through the pages, trying to distract himself from a discomfort he can't quite put a finger on.

He pauses momentarily at an article titled *'Happy Wife, Happy Life',* then continues flipping through the magazine. The intercom buzzes, and his name is called. Jack places the magazine back on the table and walks toward his therapist's office.

Inside, Miriam sits in her usual black leather chair, looking regal. She's wearing a sand-brown trouser suit, a white blouse with a plunging neckline, and pointed black heels. Her hair is tied in a ponytail, and she's seeing the world through her horn-rimmed glasses. Miriam is 37, going on 27.

She gets up and hugs Jack. The vanilla notes of her Good Girl perfume sting his nostrils as he removes his coat and settles on the light gray sofa opposite her.

"Tell me about your wife. What words would you use to describe her?" Miriam opens her notebook and begins the session.

Jack lies on his back on the sofa and runs his fingers through his short, slightly graying hair before resting his head on a white pillow to get comfortable.

"Beautiful, strong and homely," he says.

"Tell me what you mean by homely," Miriam asks?

"The upkeep of the house. It's always spotless, and meals are cooked to perfection." He pauses, then adds, "Little things too, like changing the bedsheets and the bathroom towels every week."

Miriam writes in her notebook, then sits up straight, pushing her chest outward as she does. "When you say strong, do you mean physical strength or inner strength?"

"Inner strength," Jack answers immediately.

"Tell me about a time when she demonstrated inner strength."

"She's more strong-willed than I am. When we fight, she holds her ground until I am the one initiating everything: the conversation, the apology, the intimacy."

"Have you ever told her that it bothers you?"

"My wife and I don't communicate like most couples; we speak through nonverbal codes."

Jack shifts from lying on his back to his side, his gaze wandering to Miriam's plunging neckline. Their eyes meet, and they hold the stare for a moment.

"Tell me what you mean by beautiful. Do you mean her appearance or who she is as a person?"

Jack moves back to his belly-up position and remains silent for about a minute.

"Most people find it difficult to speak poorly about their spouses, but remember, this is for your wellbeing," Miriam says, breaking the silence.

Jack stares at the ceiling for another minute.

"Tell me one negative word you would use to describe her."

"Vindictive," Jack finally says after a pause.

"Why so?"

"She does things that catch me off guard."

"Like what?"

Jack stays silent for over three minutes.

"We used to frequent this club when we started dating," he begins. "We were drinking, dancing, and having a good time when this woman with the most perfect hair came out of nowhere and stepped on Wanja's shoe. I gave her a look I often used to give her to let it slide. But instead, she took the gum she was chewing, pretended to dance with the woman, and stuck it on the back of her head.

"We ran into her again, and the poor girl had shaved her hair. Wanja had the faintest hint of a smile when she saw her bald head."

Miriam straightens up her posture, tucks a loose strand of hair behind her ear, and glances at her watch. "We've made great progress today, Jack. Let's continue this tomorrow."

Jack stands up from the sofa, and they hug again. She watches as he picks up his coat from the arm of the sofa and walks out of the door. The best way to understand someone's problems, she's found, is by seeing them through the eyes of the person closest to them. She thinks about Wanja and shivers at what she might hear next.

Wanja

An uber drops Wanja off at her house in Muthaiga, and a guard in a blue uniform opens the gate for her. She opens and closes the large oak door behind her before heading upstairs to the master bedroom. She removes her boning knife and a pink cotton dress from her bag and enters the bathroom, placing the items on the countertop. She peels off her boyish hoodie, pants, and sneakers, revealing her female form.

She gazes at her reflection in the bathroom mirror. With her innocent face, she looks like someone who could run a daycare or teach kindergarten. She looks at her body. She is short, brown and petite—though she wishes she were taller, lighter-skinned, and more curvaceous, *something more in the likeness of Miriam.* She thinks while turning on the hot water in the bathtub and picks a pack of Embassy Lights from the bathroom cabinet. She then reaches for her boning knife and places them both on the edge of the bathtub.

She slips out of her purple bra and panties, puts on a black-and-white polka-dot shower cap, turns off the faucet, drops a raspberry bath bomb that fills the tub with pink foam before stepping in.

She remembers finding Miriam's business card in one of her husband's coat pockets while doing his laundry. She had made a point to watch Miriam at a café at Warwick Center in the morning, then followed her Uber on the back of a bodaboda to Two Rivers Mall.

Anxiety churns inside her: will her husband come home to her, or will he lose himself in Miriam's arms? She reaches for her Embassy Lights, taps a cigarette from the pack and lights it. Taking a long drag, she exhales a cloud of smoke, then picks up the stainless steel boning knife. She stares at her reflection for a while before taking another pull and puffing out more smoke.

After smoking most of the cigarette, she stubs it out in the lukewarm water, climbs out of the tub, drains it, and opens the window to let the smoke escape. Jack hates it when she smokes. She had tried switching to nicotine gum for a while, but it did not do it for her—she needed the real thing.

She steps into the shower and rinses herself with cold water, then towels off, and applies lotion. Slipping into the pink cotton dress, she glances at herself in the mirror. She strikes a few poses, pretending to be Miriam, before picking up the boning knife and heading downstairs to the kitchen to prepare dinner for her husband.

She places a chopping board on the granite countertop, then cuts the chicken and dices the onions, tomatoes, red pepper, and broccoli. Once she's done, she drives the boning knife into the chopping board with a swift motion. The board is already dotted with tiny holes from previous actions.

Her husband, Jack, arrives home just as she finishes cooking—all of his middle-aged, tall, handsome, and exhausted self. As soon as he steps inside, she takes his charcoal gray coat. "How was your day, babe?" she asks cheerfully.

"Busy as usual," Jack responds with a half-smile. As the manager of a well-known chain of restaurants, he makes countless decisions every day—enough to wear out any man.

"Will you eat? I prepared chicken, rice, and a broccoli stir-fry," she offers.

Jack glances at her, shaking his head. "I'm too tired. I think I'll take a shower and call it a night."

Wanja feels resentment creeping in. How dare he cheat on her when she's given him the best of her for so long?

After Jack disappears into the bedroom, Wanja wonders if it was Miriam who drained his energy. She takes his coat, searching the pockets for receipts, then lifts it to her nose, hoping to catch a whiff of Miriam's Good Girl perfume. But all she finds is a mixture of Jack's sweat and the bergamot from his Acqua Di Gio cologne. *Maybe he cleaned up before coming home*, the thought creeps in her mind.

She remembers her plan to visit Miriam's house the following day. *Maybe, that's when it all ends,* she thinks, a slight smile playing on her lips.

Tuesday, 8th August 2023
Jack

Today, Jack is in a black suit, light brown shirt, and brown leather shoes. He shifts his weight on his seat, but the movement does little to ease his tension. He lets out a sigh as the intercom buzzes and his name is called.

He finds Miriam seated in her usual leather chair. She's dressed in a yellow blouse, and a green pencil skirt with a short slit on the side, her feet sink into avocado-green strap heels and her hair is styled in a perm. Jack marvels at her ability to look like a different woman with each session.

Miriam stands and smooths her pencil skirt, which has crept slightly above her knees, before they embrace. Jack removes his coat, lies down in his usual belly-up position on the sofa, and the session begins.

"Tell me about your wife. What words would you use to describe her?"

"Beautiful, strong, homely… and vindictive."

"Vindictive?" Miriam probes. "Have there been other incidents that have shown this side of her?"

"There have been plenty, but the one that stands out is the Uber driver incident."

Miriam opens her notebook and crosses her legs. "What happened with the Uber driver?"

Jack goes silent for a moment, as if wrestling with his conscience—whether to tell her the story or not.

"We were on our way to a friend's graduation party. I think there was some bad blood between Wanja and the driver. There are just some people you don't like, and they don't like you back. It's life."

"It started with the radio. Wanja wanted to connect her phone to the car's stereo and play her music, but the driver insisted that the car didn't have Bluetooth capability—even though we could clearly see him shuffling the music that was playing from his phone."

"I gave her the 'let it go' look, but I could tell from the glares she was shooting him in the rearview mirror that she wasn't going to let it go. Things only got worse when the driver passed our location by a block and refused to reverse, claiming he'd lose a client."

Jack shifts from his belly-up position to his side, his gaze drifting toward Miriam's legs. Her pencil skirt has ridden up from where she crossed her legs, revealing part of her thigh through the slit. Their eyes meet briefly before Jack continues.

"Wanja has this boning knife she carries around everywhere. When I ask her why, she just shrugs and says, 'A woman needs to protect herself.' When we were getting out of the car, she held the knife and ran the pointed end along the door as the driver drove off. 'A new paint job should teach him some manners,' she said as we walked to the venue. I mean, it wasn't even a five-minute walk."

Miriam uncrosses her legs, her gaze fixed on Jack.

"Besides being vindictive, what feeling does she inspire in you most of the time?"

Jack shifts back to his belly-up position, staring at the ceiling for what feels like a lifetime.

"Remember, this is for your wellbeing," Miriam gently encourages him.

"Lo… Fear," he says at last.

Wanja

WANJA TIGHTENS THE grip on the boning knife tucked into the pocket of her baggy blue denim jeans. She adjusts the hood of her black hoodie over her head and takes a drag from her Embassy Lights, while watching the maid who cleans Miriam's house. She observes as the maid buys soda and sits at the bus stop opposite Yaya Centre to drink it. Wanja flicks her cigarette into the dirt and crushes it under her black sneakers before heading toward the bench where the maid is seated.

She's been watching her for a while now. Every Tuesday afternoon, like clockwork, the maid buys a soda at the same place and sits on the same bench—without fail. After finishing, she always takes a bodaboda to the suburbs of Kileleshwa, where Miriam lives.

Wanja sits beside her. Up close, she notices that the maid's cornrows are starting to come undone at the ends. She is wearing a loose-fitting beige frock and brown rubber shoes. Wanja notices a mole on her face and how her nose looks almost like a fist. She steps on her shoelace. "Sorry," she says politely as the maid moves her feet and the lace comes undone.

The maid leaves her bottle of soda unattended on the bench next to her *kiondo* and bends over to tie her shoelace. At that moment, Wanja quickly slips two sleeping pills into the soda.

The maid sips her drink, completely unaware, while Wanja pretends to scroll through her phone. After about five minutes, the maid starts to get drowsy. Seizing the moment, Wanja moves as if to help her, picks up the *kiondo* containing the maid's uniform and job tag, then gets on a bodaboda, leaving the maid to her slumber.

Within the hour, Wanja arrives at Miriam's apartment building in Kileleshwa. She's been watching this place too. Maids here rarely last long, and there are always new faces. Keeping her hood on, Wanja heads to the ladies' washroom, and changes into the maid's baggy maroon uniform, complete with a cap, gloves, and a mask. She tightens the uniform with a belt, then walks confidently to the reception desk. Presenting the job tag, she's handed a keycard and cleaning equipment by a bored guard who barely glances at her tag. She thanks him with a cheerful hum and heads toward the elevators.

Wanja turns the lock on door number 18 on the fifth floor, and a surge of adrenaline floods her as the door to Miriam's furnished apartment closes behind her. She tosses the cleaning equipment aside and walks into the living room. She places her boning knife on the coffee table, and runs a finger over the flower vase, the artwork on the wall, and the white velvet couch.

She kneels beside the couch, pressing her nose into the rose gold cushions, stopping where Miriam's Good Girl perfume lingers the strongest. Wanja stays there for a moment, savoring the scent as if it were an intoxicating drug, before finally lifting her head, gasping for air like someone surfacing from deep water.

Rising to her feet, she heads into the American-style kitchen and makes herself a cup of tea. She returns to the living room, sits on the couch, and turns on the 55-inch TV and browses through Miriam's Netflix watchlist, she smiles as she notices they share the same taste in films. She selects *The Notebook*, the movie Miriam had been watching.

Wanja watches the film for a while, sipping her tea, before getting up and heading to the bedroom.

She runs a finger along the edge of Miriam's queen bed and lets her hands run through the rose gold pillows and white duvet before stepping into the walk-in closet. She marvels at all the clothes and shoes on display.

One by one, she picks out outfits and pairs of shoes to try on. She undresses, rummages through the drawers until she finds what she's looking for. She sinks her nose into Miriam's Victoria's Secret panties and keeps her nose in them for a while before coming up for air. Then she selects several matching bra and underwear sets to try on.

Wanja models the underwear and loose-fitting dresses in front of the mirror, mimicking Miriam's movements and giggling like a teenager. After a while, she removes the shoes pinching her feet and the clothes, then hops into the shower.

After cleaning herself, Wanja slips into Miriam's bathrobe and climbs into her queen bed, turning this way and that while running her hands through the pillows and bedsheets. It's the watch on the bedside table that jolts her out of her stupor. She glances at it and realizes she's been in the house for over three hours. The maid's sleeping pills should be wearing off soon, and she needs ample time to prepare dinner for her husband.

Wanja quickly changes back into her maid's uniform, tidies up the house, picks up her cleaning equipment, and heads for the door. She stops for a moment, then rushes back into the house, gripping her boning knife tightly as she approaches the door.

Wednesday, 9th August 2023
Jack

JACK PACES SLOWLY in the waiting area of his therapist's office at noon as the intercom buzzes and his name is called. He is dressed in a blue pinstripe suit, a white shirt, and blue loafers. Miriam is in a figure-hugging gray dress that cuts above her knees, and her feet sink into cream ankle boots. Her hair remains in the same perm, but her eyes are behind Ray-Ban glasses. Jack admires her sense of style as they hug and settle on their seats.

"Tell me about your wife. What words would you use to describe her?" Miriam asks as she opens her notebook, beginning their session.

"Beautiful, strong, homely, and vindictive," Jack replies, after removing his coat and adjusting himself on the sofa so that he's staring at the ceiling.

"What feeling does she inspire in you most of the time?"

"Fear."

"Tell me an instance when she has made you afraid," Miriam says, tugging at the hem of her dress, which climbs up with her every movement.

Jack stares at the ceiling for what feels like a lifetime and then begins.

"We had this maid for a long time. She was a great maid. She would keep the house as clean as Wanja wanted, and to top it off, she had her own recipe book. We almost had a chef in our kitchen," Jack goes silent, his gaze still fixed on the ceiling.

"Wanja discovered that the maid was wearing her clothes while she was away," Jack continues after what feels like five minutes. "I told her they were just clothes. 'Heavens, we should give her your entire wardrobe for the job she does in the kitchen alone,' I said, but Wanja wasn't listening. She said the maid was trying to compete with her, and from the look in her eye, I knew she wasn't going to let it slide. Only, I wasn't prepared for what she did next."

Miriam shifts her weight and pulls down the hem of her dress.

"I came from work one evening, unlocked the door, and immediately heard muffled screams coming from our bedroom. I rushed there and stood rooted to the spot for a whole minute, astonished by what my wife was doing to our maid."

"She had stripped her naked, handcuffed both her hands to the window grille, and gagged her mouth with a cloth. Wanja had her pack of Embassy Lights beside her; she kept lighting a cigarette and using the maid's bareback to put it out. You know what scared me even more?" Jack pauses as Miriam shakes her head. "She just glanced at me and continued."

Miriam moves uneasily on her leather chair, tugging at the hem of her dress.

"The whole house smelled like burnt meat. I think she had been doing it to her all day. I had to pay her a hefty sum to keep her mouth shut. I suppose she never did, because no other maid has agreed to work for us since."

Thursday, 10th August 2023
Wanja

WANJA WAKES UP at 6:00 a.m. and looks at the emptiness next to her. Jack has been leaving early lately; *is he avoiding her?* She wonders. She picks up her phone from the bedside stand and runs a hand through his side of the bed. It's cold. Her jaw tightens. She's starting to hate him. How dare he betray her like this when she has given him her all?

She opens her Instagram and taps on Miriam's profile, scrolling through it with excitement. She sent her a follow request long ago, and it has only now been accepted. *This is a new level of intimacy between them,* she thinks, while going through Miriam's photos, which portray a confident woman whose hard work has rewarded her with a good living that allows her to have expensive taste.

She fights the urge to like all of them. She likes one where she is wearing a yellow dress and comments on the latest one, where she has red lipstick. *I'm in love with your style, honey.* She writes before bookmarking both of them, deciding to go looking for the outfit and lipstick in the stores, later in the day.

She taps on Miriam's recent stories. Miriam is seated on her couch in a white bathrobe, towel wrapped around her head, talking about how her maid was drugged by an unknown person and how insecurity has skyrocketed in Nairobi. As she gets up to go to the bedroom, Wanja notices a newly installed CCTV camera. *It's strange that she was in that house not long ago: in that same bed, wearing her clothes, feeling the way she does every day of her life.* She gets a head rush from the thought alone and taps to the next story.

It's an easy do-it-yourself hair tutorial. Wanja gets out of bed and ties her hair in a ponytail, just like Miriam. Then she realizes she doesn't have the products Miriam is using, and decides to buy them when she goes shopping. She taps on the next story; it's Miriam's makeup routine. She decides she will get her makeup set too as she goes to make breakfast.

After breakfast, she goes shopping and returns in the afternoon with her bags. She slips out of her clothes and soaks in the tub with her raspberry bath bomb, Embassy Lights and boning knife. Afterward, she rinses off in the shower and puts on the yellow dress she just bought. She does her makeup and hair just like Miriam and finishes by applying red lipstick. She looks in the mirror and gasps, "Hi Miriam?"

Wanja picks up her phone from the table and opens Instagram. Miriam has a new story. She will be attending a breakfast event on women's social issues at a high-end hotel the next day. Wanja opens a new tab and loads the event's website. There are three slots remaining.

She finds herself signing up for the event and pledging 200,000 Kenya shillings to the cause—knowing all too well Jack won't be happy when he notices such a hefty amount missing from their joint account. She confirms the time and enters it into her calendar. A mix of dread and excitement washes over her. Tomorrow, she will meet Miriam—the woman she's been watching. The woman her husband has been cheating on her with.

Friday, 11th August 2023
Miriam

WANJA DRIVES HER Honda CR-V into the basement parking lot of Movenpick Hotel at 10:00 a.m. Jack had bought it for her on her 30th birthday as a gift for their seven-year anniversary, which, counting this year, now marks 10 years together. She shifts the gear into park and changes from the flats she uses for driving into red pumps. She's wearing a black bob wig and a slim-fitting black dress that makes her look like a school teacher.

She picks up her red handbag—with her boning knife inside—and heads for the lifts. In the lift, she's a bundle of nerves, stricken with fear at the thought of meeting Miriam. This woman she has been watching for as long as she can remember is about to finally meet her. The lift dings and opens onto the hotel's ground floor. She steps out and walks to the reception area.

"Hello, my name is Wanja. I am here for the Women's Social Issues breakfast meeting." As she says it, she realizes it's a mouthful.

The receptionist looks for her name on the computer while wearing her job's most important piece of attire; a plastic smile.

"Oh, the WSI breakfast meeting," the receptionist says after spotting Wanja's name next to the 200,000 Kenya shillings pledge. "It's on the first floor, opposite the lobby. Do you need a bellboy to assist you?"

"I'm okay, thank you," Wanja replies as she heads to the lifts again.

The lift opens on the first floor, and she spots the sign for the breakfast meeting almost immediately. She considers ducking into the ladies' washroom to calm her nerves but finds herself pushing the door open and stepping into the meeting room instead. A waitress at the entrance asks for her name and directs her to her table.

Seated, Wanja cranes her neck, searching for Miriam. She finally spots her talking to two other women. Instinctively, she opens her handbag and grips the boning knife inside and her nerves start to ease.

She watches as Miriam walks toward the podium to give her speech and sees what her husband, Jack, must see. Miriam exudes a poise and grace that's rare. Her hair is styled in a ponytail, and she's dressed in a peach pleated skirt, a white blouse, and black red bottom heels. She looks like an ambassador's wife—a look Wanja could never pull off, not even on her best day.

Lost in thought, Wanja doesn't realize Miriam has finished her speech until she's startled by her own name being called: "…Wanja, our esteemed guest. Let's welcome her with a round of applause."

She should have kept her donation modest, she thinks, embarrassed, while getting up and walking to the podium. "Our girls mean everything to me," she begins after introducing herself as a housewife with a passion for women's empowerment.

"I was once a girl in the village without sanitary towels, and I wouldn't wish that on any girl." The lie slips out effortlessly, surprising even her. "If giving the little I have means girls everywhere can be comfortable and confident enough to chase their dreams, then it's the least I can do." The room erupts in applause as she steps down from the podium.

Miriam approaches her, and the scent of vanilla from her Good Girl perfume envelopes Wanja as they embrace.

"Thank you for the donation. It will go a long way," Miriam says after they hug.

"Don't mention it. It's the least I can do."

"Your story is moving. It could inspire a lot of girls."

"You know, I've always been interested in women's issues. We're all we've got."

"Perhaps we could grab a cup of coffee and talk more about it," Miriam suggests, unknowingly taking the bait.

"Or maybe we could have brunch at my place… Sorry, you must be wondering who is this strange woman who invites someone she barely knows to her home?"

"No, not at all. We are a sisterhood," Miriam replies, handing Wanja her business card.

Wanja gets into her handbag and spots the boning knife, her fingers brushing against its handle for a moment. "I'm sorry, I can never seem to find anything in my bag," she says, passing Miriam her card, which has her name and phone number. She had ordered them back when she used to accompany Jack to business events, having grown tired of being asked for her card and pulling out her phone instead.

Miriam laughs as she takes the card. "It's a miracle we find anything at all."

"Tell me about it," Wanja giggles. "How is your weekend? We could do a Sunday afternoon," she suggests, feeling a spark of courage.

Miriam thumbs through her Galaxy Note and checks her schedule. "You're in luck. I'm free this Sunday."

"Perfect!" Wanja replies, the hint of a smile playing on her lips.

After the breakfast meeting, Wanja settles into her CR-V, changing from her pumps into her flats. As she pulls out of the parking lot, she reflects on the fact that she has just spoken to the woman her husband has been cheating on her with. Now, it's time to discover what she is truly made of.

Sunday, 13ᵗʰ August 2023
Wanja

THE GUARD OPENS the gate. Miriam drives her Mercedes up the driveway into Wanja's compound. Earlier, Wanja had gone through the trouble of parking Jack's Range Rover behind their house, leaving only her CR-V in the compound.

Miriam is met at the door by a delighted Wanja, who is wearing a pink dress and black red bottom heels with her hair styled in a ponytail.

"You clean up nicely for a Sunday," Miriam says while handing her a bottle of wine. Her hair is freshly braided, and she's in Levi's jeans, white sneakers, and a waterfall cardigan.

"I try," Wanja says, picking up the wine and welcoming Miriam to her house. "I'm sorry if I'm too excited. I have been looking forward to our little date the whole morning," she giggles.

"I couldn't sleep either," Miriam jokes as she takes a seat at the dining table.

There is freshly squeezed lemonade, mango juice, and passion fruit juice on the table. A flask with milk and another with yogurt sit nearby. Trays of sausages, bacon, chocolate croissants, pineapples, strawberries, and watermelon are also present.

"This is quite a setup. Are you expecting more guests?"

"Not really. Just making sure we don't starve to death in case we lose track of time."

Miriam laughs faintly. "So tell me, when did you start your women-empowerment journey?"

"Let's save that for later," Wanja says. "I love your sweater. Tell me where you shop, what your hobbies are, and where you travel. I want to be exactly like you."

"Oh, this old thing? It's just something I found at the back of my wardrobe and threw on." Miriam laughs, getting into the girl talk.

"If that's the case, I want to live in the back of your wardrobe," Wanja says as she gets up to serve her. "Mango, passion or lemonade," she asks?

"Lemonade is just fine."

Wanja pours her a glass and brushes her elbow against Miriam's side boob. Miriam shifts uncomfortably and places a croissant and some bacon on her plate.

"This is a big house. Do you live alone?" She immediately regrets asking, realizing she might be a widow.

"Something like that," Wanja replies.

After parking Jack's Range Rover at the back of the house, she had removed all their wedding photos from the walls. "You should try the strawberries; they are farm to table." She reaches for one, dips it in yogurt, and brings it toward Miriam's mouth.

Miriam moves away. "I will try them later." She looks at her watch; it's 1:30 p.m. "I won't be long; I have a thing in the next 30 minutes or so."

"But you just got here!"

Miriam stays silent now, noticing that Wanja has done her makeup and hair exactly how she does, and the perfume, pink dress and shoes she's wearing are similar to the ones she owns.

"I had so much planned for us. But if you're leaving early, I'll be forced to skip to the grand finale, won't I?" she teases.

"Grand finale?"

"Yes. The part where I confess my love for you and make a grand gesture to prove it."

"I really have to get going," Miriam says as she stands up.

"It will only take a second. Follow me to the kitchen."

Miriam hesitates, following her from a distance.

"Come on, I won't bite," Wanja giggles.

The moment they enter the kitchen, Miriam starts screaming.

There is broken glass everywhere and a long trail of red. Jack is lying in a pool of blood where the red stops, with Wanja's boning knife sunk deep in his neck.

"Now there's nothing stopping us from being together," Wanja says, with a big smile.

"Call an ambulance!" Miriam screams. "Call an ambulance!"

"He's gone; it's me and you against the world now, Miriam."

Miriam screams until the guard at the gate storms into the house. She keeps screaming long after the police take Wanja away until her voice is hoarse.

Monday, 4th September 2023
Miriam

MIRIAM LOCKS HER furnished apartment in Kileleshwa at 8:00 a.m. and takes the lifts to the parking lot. She is wearing an ivory belted skirt suit. The skirt cuts above her knees, and the front slit runs to the middle of her thigh. Her heels make a tapping sound as she walks to her Mercedes Benz.

She enters the car, and picks up her Galaxy Note before turning on the ignition, and takes a selfie. Her hair is a long weave with bangs, and she sees the world through Zara eyewear. *This hair and these glasses are giving me life,* she captions the story and posts it, then turns on the ignition and puts the gear to drive.

She's in her office in Gigiri within the hour, drinking tea and going through the day's newspaper. The story is a short paragraph on the back pages: *Wanja has been admitted at Mathari Mental Hospital, awaiting transfer to Langata Women's Prison.*

She flips through the newspaper and sees a tribute to Jack by the company he worked for. It's strange to her that he was lying opposite her not too long ago, sharing a conversation, and now he's no more. She folds the newspaper in half before placing it on her desk, readying herself for her client.

She has met him before in an introductory therapy session, and she has been looking forward to their sessions since. She glances at his file again: tall, handsome, with a classic flair about him, and newly married. She sits in her leather chair and hears the lock on her office door turn. Miriam smiles pleasantly and gets up to hug him.

The tobacco in his Tom Ford cologne stings her nose as she directs him to the sofa, where he sits with his legs apart. She crosses hers, and the slit in her skirt exposes her bare thigh. He looks at her. She holds his gaze for a moment before speaking.

"Tell me about your wife. What words would you use to describe her?" Miriam asks as she opens her notebook, ready to begin their session.

One Last Job

The sun was going down in Kangemi, and you could hear the drums in Makau's compound. Six men and five women of the cloth were singing and praying barefoot in their white *akurinu* gowns. Some danced, others jumped, and a few spoke in tongues.

Makau's wife, Eva, a striking brown-skinned woman who had just turned 26, was in the house preparing supper and refreshments. They had agreed long ago that she would not be part of the congregation. It was a small price to pay. When she had found out what the gathering was a front for, Makau had feared she would pack her bags and leave. But she had stayed, and Makau had loved her more for it.

The crescendo of the drums rose higher. "*Mungu tunakuabudu. Wewe ndiye mwanzo na mwisho; kama si wewe, tungekuwa wapi?*" one of the male congregants chanted, his masculine arms lifted up to the sky—the sky that was now lit by the stars and the moon.

"Eeeeeiih!" a woman wailed like a banshee and started hopping on one leg, the other leg swinging in the air. "Eeeeei-ih!" The drums thumped and she threw herself onto the dirt. *"Roboboshanti shintarababoshi!"* she chanted, rolling around and speaking her gibberish. *"Roboboshanti shintarababoshi!"*

It was almost midnight when the worship quieted. Eva came out barefoot, wearing a long purple pleated dress and white turban, carrying cups of tea, a thermos, and loaves of bread. After refreshments, believers dispersed, and Eva went back to the house, but four of them stayed behind: three bulky men and a thin woman—Makau, Simiyu, Kim and Njeri.

"Simiyu, you keep worshiping like that, and the white smoke will rise at the Vatican, announcing you as our new pope," joked Kim, a short, dark-skinned man with wide nostrils. The group, huddled together, broke into laughter. Their chatter was soon drowned out by Njeri, who walked around the compound, beating her drum and singing her *kigooco* loudly.

"Did you bring everything we need for the operation?" Makau glanced at Kim after the laughter died down, then checked his Casio watch. 12:45 a.m. Sun 19th Jan 2003, it read.

Kim unzipped a small, white bag he'd been dancing with all night and revealed three black pistols with the serial numbers filed off.

"Right here, boss."

"Where do we stand with the ambassador? Have you gotten hold of his schedule?" He was looking at Simiyu—a tall, light skinned man who was easy on the eyes and light on his feet. Makau had always felt uneasy around him and had made a point of keeping him close.

"I managed to tap his secretary's phone. He's scheduled to leave the country this weekend. That's when we hit his house."

"One last job, boys. Let's do it right." The three big men adjourned their meeting. Njeri, with her drum and her *kigooco* continued for another 10 minutes before quieting down.

Makau entered his unevenly cemented, three-room wooden house. There was the sitting room that doubled as the kitchen, and two bedrooms—one for him and Eva, and the other for their kids. Eva had warmed some water and put it in a basin in their bedroom, which was illuminated by a kerosene lamp. Makau used a damp cloth to clean himself before changing into a fresh white gown, turban, and sandals. He stepped out of the house and poured the water in the toilet, which also doubled as the bathroom.

When he returned, Eva had set his food on the table and was staring at him with sad, brown eyes. "This is a small town, and people talk," she said as Makau sat down on an old brown sofa and untied his white turban without a word, revealing a bald head with a scar that ran from his forehead to the middle of his scalp. He kept his head shaved to the bone. He was in a line of work that required agility and he didn't need hair weighing him down. He placed the turban beside him. His wife went to the kitchen section of their sitting room and came back with warm water and a clean towel for his hands.

She looked at him again with those sad, big, brown eyes, and Makau remembered when they began dating. What he loved most about her was that she was a throwback. She dressed the way women from his mother's era did—long frocks and a *kamisi* underneath. He had gasped the first time he saw her naked; such a beautiful body hidden under so much fabric. She was a throwback even as a wife—meeting him at the door with hot food, washing his hands, making sure the kids were clean and fed before bedtime—and she did it all without complaining or reminding him about changing times.

"Makau, this is a very small town," she repeated, her voice full of concern. As a gust of wind blew through a crack in the wood, and the kerosene lamp on the table flickered. Makau pinched a big chunk of *ugali* with his fat hand, scooped up some *sukuma* and meat from his plate. He chewed and swallowed, his Adam's apple doing an up-and-down jig.

"It's a small town, and we provide religious services for it," he boomed mid-chew.

"How long will they be fooled?" His wife lowered her voice to a whisper. "What about our ki…" She stopped herself. The message was home.

Makau wiped his plate clean, and Eva handed him a damp towel to wipe his hands. He wasn't annoyed or irritated by her questions; they had this conversation every week. She was just a concerned woman. He stood up, picked the kerosene lamp from their bedroom, and walked with it to his kids' bedroom.

There were two beds, one on each corner of the room. He sat on the plastic Kenpoly chair that was in the center— the same one he sat on every night to read them a bedtime story. Only when his work called on him, would he find them asleep, and it ate him inside.

He picked *The Lion King* Ladybird storybook from the shelf and read it slowly as his children breathed softly in their sleep. His eyes grew glassy, and he paused, closing the book momentarily before resuming. When he was done, he returned the book on the shelf, kissed both his seven-year-old son and nine-year-old daughter on the forehead, picked up the lamp, and went back to the bedroom where his wife lay waiting.

"One last job, and I'm done," he whispered. He kissed her gently on the lips, turned off the lamp with a puff, and pulled the covers to his head.

Eva didn't ask about details of the job. When she stayed up at night, she tried to imagine that her husband did honorable work, that he was an engineer working a night shift at an electric company. But even then, her mind would wander to visions of blood and bullet holes. The only solace she found was knowing that her husband was good at what he did. They called him "Sharpshooter" for a reason, and perhaps it was why he had survived this long. But she also knew that every dog had its day. *One last job.* She clutched the words like sand in her hands as sleep took her.

The Hit

"*ROBOBOSHANTI SHINTARABABOSHI!*" a woman wailed like a banshee and threw herself onto the ground.

"*Shintarababoshi!*" a man echoed, mirroring the gibberish. The drums grew louder, filling the air as the congregation sang, danced, and prayed in their white *akurinu* gowns. When the clock struck midnight, Eva emerged barefoot in a long pleated green dress and white turban, carrying cups of tea, a thermos, and loaves of bread. After the refreshments, the believers dispersed. Eva returned inside, while outside, Njeri's drumbeats and *kigooco* rose to a crescendo.

"We hit the ambassador's house tonight," Kim announced, putting on his brown loafers. "He left on Friday for dignitary work."

"Did you get the blueprints?" Makau asked, lacing up his black leather shoes.

"The safe is upstairs, in his study," Kim confirmed.

"The vests and masks?"

"Everything we need is in the car, a kilometer from here."

Makau turned to Simiyu. "What about the power?"

"I will cut the power and the entire Runda suburb will go dead," Simiyu said, pulling the tongue of his second black sneaker into place. "You'll have 15, maybe 20 seconds to break into the house before the backup generator kicks in. Once inside, you can disconnect the alarm and surveillance."

"And the guards?" Kim asked.

"They won't know we're there. But if they do…" Simiyu folded his hand into the shape of a gun, mimed two shots, then puckered his lips and blew the tips of his fore and middle finger.

They ran through the plans one last time, switching roles and revisiting each detail. In their line of work, things were unpredictable. Every team member needed to know every detail of the operation in case something happened to one of them and someone had to step in and adapt.

When they felt confident in their plans, Makau got up and entered his house as Njeri's drumbeats and *kigooco* echoed into the night. He lit a kerosene lamp and moved quietly to his kids' bedroom. He sat on his usual Kenpoly chair and opened *The Lion King* Ladybird storybook, reading softly as his children slept peacefully. Two silver rivers formed on his cheeks, which he quickly wiped with the back of his hand and closed the book. He made to return it to the shelf, but thought otherwise and put it in his pocket instead. He then kissed his seven-year-old and nine-year-old on their foreheads. He did not know it then but it would be a long time before he was able to kiss them again.

As he headed out, Makau glanced at his wife, catching her sad, brown eyes. "One last job," he whispered, brushing a kiss on her lips before slipping into the night.

The three middle-aged men walked in silence under the moonlight toward a gray, 1995 Toyota Starlet parked by the side of an empty road. Kim took the driver's seat. Simiyu opened and closed the back left door for Makau, then joined Kim on the passenger seat. They shed their *akurinu* gowns into black hoodies and trousers. The engine purred to life, and the Starlet vanished into the distance.

They slowed to a halt near an electric transformer in Runda Estate. "Simiyu, you're coming with me. Kim, kill the power and be on the lookout." Makau always reserved the final operation details for the very last minute to avoid betrayal. They tucked their pistols into their waistbands, rolled out of the car, opened the boot and came out with black masks, gloves and a pull-up ladder. Within five minutes, they were behind the ambassador's wall, waiting for the signal.

The lights went off and within a split-second, they were over the wall. "Hurry," Makau signaled to Simiyu after he opened the lock to the back door. Simiyu hesitated. Makau proceeded inside the house, deciding he would deal with his insolence later. He disconnected the alarm and surveillance and climbed the stairs quickly and stealthily toward the ambassador's study where the safe was.

As soon as he turned the lock and pushed open the door to the study, the lights and alarm blazed on, and Makau found himself face-to-face with a police officer in blue, his gun trained at his temples. Behind the officer, the Australian ambassador sat in his plush leather chair, behind his mahogany desk, impeccably dressed in a black suit, not a single hair out of place, as though this were a regular status meeting.

Makau's reflexes took over. Before the officer could decide whether to pull the trigger or arrest him, Makau's Glock was in hand, and he fired. The bullet struck the officer's neck, sending him to the floor clutching the spurting wound. The ambassador, realizing he was now in danger, fumbled for a gun in his desk drawer, but he never reached it. One shot, and his brains were splattered all over his mahogany desk.

Makau dashed down the stairs, taking out a guard at the back door as he leapt over the fence and sprinted to the Toyota Starlet. Kim lay slumped over the steering wheel, lifeless. Simiyu was gone. Cold dread settled in Makau's chest as he realized he had been betrayed. Now, he had to disappear, before the world closed in on him.

Six Years Passed

No one recognized Makau—except for his wife, Eva. He now had a mane of hair covering his once-bald scalp, hiding the scar that had once marked him. The once robust man, built like a *mugumo* tree, had grown pale, and his jacket and trousers now hung loosely on his frame—a result of always being on the run.

After news broke of the deaths of the Australian ambassador and two police officers, there was nowhere he could hide. Things worsened after a bounty of 1 million Kenya shillings was placed on his head, forcing him to cross the border into Somalia.

He had traveled to Garissa, staying in the remote village of Ijara, where he dressed in a *kanzu* and *keffiyeh* to blend in with the locals, posing as a shopkeeper. But he was all over the news; after only a month, a customer recognized him, forcing him to flee into Boni forest and cross the Somali border through the dense Badana-Bushbush forest into Kismayo. It was a tumultuous journey, and without his sharpshooter skills, the bandits would have claimed his life.

In Kismayo, he rented a single-room house and became a fisherman. He thought of starting a new family, but every time he tried, memories of his wife and children came flooding back, stopping him. Each night before bed, he opened *The Lion King* Ladybird storybook and read it, imagining the world as Scar, himself as Mufasa, and his children as Simba. When he finished, he kissed his pillowcase twice before falling asleep.

In his sixth year away, something happened. Perhaps it was an epiphany, or maybe, after all these years, he felt his heat had faded. It could also have been his loneliness consuming him, the thought of wanting to embrace his wife and children clouding his judgment. He returned as a Somali refugee through Dadaab, sneaking out of the camp with the little money he had earned as a fisherman. From there, he made his way to Garissa town, and finally, to Nairobi.

The first person he visited was Simiyu, who lived in a one-bedroom house in Buruburu. It was on a Thursday evening, and Simiyu was lounging on the sofa watching TV, unaware, as Makau quietly picked the lock on his door. The clock on the wall read 5:30 p.m., and the calendar showed Thursday, 3rd September 2009. When Makau entered, the only sound Simiyu heard was a sudden crack as Makau twisted his head, breaking his neck and killing him instantly.

Next, he went to his house in Kangemi. His wife, Eva, met him with an uncertain embrace—unsure of who he had become, and unsure about her own future. After embracing, Makau held her hands and looked at her. In her white turban, blue pleated dress, and slippers, he felt deep relief that the woman he knew was still here for him. Then, he moved toward his children's room. He had missed them. He had even missed the Sunday evening congregants. *Roboboshanti shintarababoshi!* The memory made him smile as he held the handle to their bedroom door and gently pushed it open.

"They're in boarding school," his wife, Eva, said hesitantly, trying to shield him from the inevitable truth that was sleeping in the room.

Things had changed, yet felt strangely familiar. Beside the two beds where his children once slept was a baby cot. Inside was a child who couldn't have been older than three. The toddler giggled as Makau approached. "I'm sorry, Makau," Eva began, her voice barely above a whisper. "I was lonely, and I needed support, and Simuyu was there. I thought… I thought I'd never see you again. I swear, if I'd known you'd come back, I wouldn't have invited him to my bed."

Makau didn't feel anger or resentment. Perhaps, after all his years of crime, this was his punishment. He reached into his coat pocket and took out *The Lion King* Ladybird storybook. The Kenpoly chair was still in the same spot, untouched. "The children didn't want it removed," Eva murmured. Makau sat down and began reading the storybook to the child in the cot. His eyes turned glassy, and trails of silver streamed down his cheeks, the weight of his deeds pressing heavily upon him. He hadn't reached halfway through the story when a loud bang sounded at the door. Eva's mouth opened to scream, but before the sound could come out, five military soldiers flooded into the room.

"We're here for the sharpshooter," one of them boomed. Makau didn't resist. After six years of looking over his shoulder, he was ready for it to end. He closed the storybook, slipped it into his coat pocket, and raised his hands. He kissed the boy in the cot on the forehead, then kissed his wife on the lips as the soldiers cuffed him and led him away.

Makau sat in his cell, dressed in light blue striped prison garb and red slippers, awaiting his death sentence, but it never came. Instead, a fat police officer in green and black boots appeared, carrying a black briefcase, and handed it to Makau. Inside was a pistol and a piece of paper bearing the name of the opposition leader. The fat police officer looked at him. "Nod your head if you understand."

Makau nodded.

"Follow me."

The sun had set, and the police station was lit by fluorescent tubes. They walked through the parking lot and stopped beside a dark Toyota Noah without number plates. The police officer handed him the keys. "I expect you back here tomorrow morning with the job done, or there will be four bullets with your family's names on them."

Makau returned to a new cell. It had a comfortable bed, a small fridge with refreshments, a sofa, and a TV. On the bed lay new clothes: an orange sweater, blue trousers, black leather shoes, and two white shirts. The nine o'clock news appeared on the TV screen: OPPOSITION LEADER GUNNED DOWN BY UNKNOWN GUNMEN. The news anchor, with her heavily made-up face, long false eyelashes, and low-cut dress, spoke somberly. Makau sighed, switched off the TV, and changed into his new clothes. He had a midday visit scheduled with his family.

"Where is the other child?" he asked his wife after hugging his two children.

"I thought… I didn't think you would want to see him," Eva stammered.

"Bring him next time."

Makau reached into his pocket and came out with the Ladybird storybook. After he was done reading to his children, he kissed each of them on the forehead and his wife on the lips.

"Makau, I received a lot of cash in our joint bank account. It came from an unknown source. What's happening?" Eva whispered.

"They asked for my details… so that's what that was about?" Makau mumbled to himself. "Eva, I feel my time coming soon. Take care of the children. And take care of yourself," he added.

In the months that followed, there were minor jobs that didn't make headlines; a troublesome city councilman vanished, a civilian witness set to testify in a wealthy man's case drowned in Nairobi River the day before the hearing, a government whistleblower fell and broke her neck while ziplining.

Eva sometimes visited Makau alone, and they shared time together in his cell quarters as husband and wife. "I can feel my time coming soon. Take care of my children. Take care of yourself," Makau always reminded her. When she brought the children, he would read them the Ladybird storybook, kiss their foreheads, and then kiss her on the lips.

Before the year was over, the fat police officer appeared at his cell again with the same dark briefcase. Inside, was a rope tied into the shape of a noose and a note. They walked to the parking lot, where an ink-blue Nissan Sylphy without number plates waited. The police officer handed him the keys. As he sat in the Nissan, Makau stared at the note, unable to shake off the weight of the name written there.

The following morning, after the job, Makau ate his breakfast as usual, though he thought it tasted funny. There was a lot of commotion and noise in the prison. He glanced at the TV in the cafeteria. It was 10:00 a.m., Monday, 16th August 2010. The news headlines flashed across the screen: PRIME MINISTER FOUND DEAD IN SUSPECTED SUICIDE AT KITUSURU HOME. Makau returned to his cell, feeling a slight headache and nausea creeping in. By midday, the headache had escalated into a migraine, and he'd vomited all his breakfast until he was now vomiting blood.

"Guards!" he screamed, holding the cell bars. No one answered. He convulsed, coughing up a final spurt of blood before collapsing lifeless onto his bed, his head coming to rest against *The Lion King* Ladybird storybook he'd once read so fondly to his children.

"ROBOBOSHANTI SHINTARABABOSHI!" a woman wailed like a banshee. *"Shintarababoshi!"* a man echoed, mirroring the gibberish. The drums thundered louder in Makau's compound as the congregation sang, danced, and prayed, dressed in their white *akurinu* garb, as Eva led them through worship under the watchful glow of the midnight moon.

Fools Die

Andrea

I was born a rich girl in a family of three children. But that's not my superpower. My superpower is that I can tell within the first minute of interacting with a man whether or not he's a fool.

Most men have a terrible secret: they are fools. You will see them walking with swagger and occupying rooms with confidence, but it's arrogance. After they get a deep voice, broad shoulders, and a standing penis for every passing skirt, they think they are conquerors. God forbid they get a bit of money; then they believe they have unlocked luminary status.

I have a superpower of picking out a fool within a minute of interacting with a man, so I knew when I had landed a good one. But there was one problem. You see, Joseph was not well off. He was a mechanic who lived in a shack and drove a jalopy, but I saw his kindness, charm, and erudition. I saw a man who did not wear hubris like a second skin and feel accomplished for it. But my parents would have none of it.

They raised an eyebrow and whispered between themselves when I introduced him. He didn't look the way our inner circle did: like money. To me, money was secondary; you could stumble upon it any day, but you couldn't just find a man like Joseph around the corner. Besides, there is a cure for being broke, but there is no cure for fools. There isn't a hospital in the world that can treat it. It's malignant, and the only cure is cutting it down and throwing it away.

I pulled my mom aside—an elegant woman whose nickname was "The Duchess"—and brought this up. "Andrea, don't be ridiculous. You can put a monkey in a suit, but you can't buy it class. Honey, please don't make us the butt of jokes and innuendo. You have had your fun; now do away with him," she brushed me off brusquely. It was my fault. I expected too much from a woman who had gotten married to a fool.

My brother married a governor's daughter. My sister married a CEO's son. I was set to marry the president of a clothing company, but, like most men, he turned out to be a fool.

I had visited the house once or twice—a mansion with a bevy of maids—yet he still dropped hints that he wanted me to take care of him. I had spent a weekend at my sister's matrimonial home to understand what he meant: cooking for him, doing his laundry, and waiting with a pot of hot food on those late nights when he staggered home after visiting his mistress. I was nobody's maid; what made him think I would become his slave?

My sister had beamed when she first introduced her fiancé to us. I mean, my parents arranged it, but she acted as if it was new stuff. I could only guess that they had already slept together and that the sex was good—good, but was it enough for her to agree to slavery? I did my part. I used my superpower. His regal manner and eloquence did not fool me, not once, not when I had been seeing through men like him for years. Yes, he had a straight 'A' in blithering fool.

I pulled her to the side and told her it was better for her to be a damsel in distress all her life than to sup with a buffoon, but she didn't listen—not when the sex was good—good.

"Why do you always have to ruin everything?"

"Mind your own business."

"You're too young to understand these things."

These were the words that she kept throwing in my face when I tried to make her see reason.

More than once during my visit, I heard her whimpering in her room. When I asked, she claimed something had gotten into her eye. I didn't know that having something in your eye made tears and mucus run in rivers down your nostrils and your body convulse with hiccups. But my point was clear: you could not fight the superpower—it was disturbingly accurate.

I pulled my dad to the side—a towering man with graying hair—and shared my concerns.

"Andrea, you know we don't just marry anybody in this house. Marriages, for us, transcend love. They are about strengthening our family empire. You have to get this mechanic out of your head."

"But that's the thing—I can't get him out of my head," I said defiantly.

My dad gripped my arm, his nails digging into my skin, nearly drawing blood. "You will do what we tell you to do," he barked.

"I'll run away with him before I marry one of your arrangements," I heard myself roar. "I refuse to be moved like a pawn on some board for your selfish whims." I wretched my arm free from his grip.

My parents knew I was willful, but even I didn't anticipate what they did next. My boyfriend was plucked from his humble mechanic shop in the ghetto and given an apprenticeship at the dealership of one of my dad's friends. A year later, he was the managing director of the company, and the year after that, we were in church saying our wedding vows before the eyes of God and men.

And then he became a fool.

Joseph

I WAS BORN a poor boy in a family of eleven children, but that's not my superpower. My superpower is knowing my place. The world lies to all of us, convincing us that ambition is a beautiful thing when, in truth, it's dangerous. I've read enough books to fear ambition. Starting with *The Great Gatsby*, many foolish men have met their ruin in its hands.

Before Andrea, I didn't entertain illusions of grandeur. I had no desire for wealth or status, and in some way, I believed it made me happier. I embraced my role as a humble mechanic. I woke up each morning, took a cold bath from my faded blue basin, had my sugarless tea with yams, and drove to my shop in my beat-up 1972 Datsun.

I would have married a Class Eight drop out—Form Four, if I got lucky—and together we'd have six or nine children. I would have worked tirelessly in my small shop to provide for them, oblivious of ambition or any shiny temptation to lure me from my place. That was before Andrea showed up in her Mercedes S-Class, then kept returning, even when her car didn't have an issue.

At first, I thought someone might jump from the bushes with cameras to tell me it was a prank and I was on some live TV show. But no one came, and she kept coming around. Eating *ugali* and *sukuma wiki* with me at my favorite *kibanda*, staying a minute longer in my shop—dusting, arranging my tools, and helping manage my cash flows.

I was dizzy the first time she took me to one of her family events. I marveled at the opulence with my mouth wide open. It lit a flame in my imagination, and for the first time, I realized life could offer a whole lot more than I had settled for. I didn't even mind when her sister, with a face drenched in mockery, looked me up and down and sneered, "I see you've settled for one of our servants. What is he, the janitor?"

After a few events and a couple of dates in upscale hotels, I got spoiled. My sugarless tea and my yams started tasting horrible. I could no longer bear cold showers, the absence of air conditioning in my Datsun, and the deafening noise in my shop gave me migraines. It was a breath of fresh air when her father came to my shop with an offer that felt like a dream. "You must worship a living God because your life is about to change, Son," he said with a poker face, but I couldn't hide the excitement on mine. I wasn't just going to taste ambition; I was about to feast on it.

Things were rosy for a year or so after I wed Andrea. The changes didn't come all at once but crept in, little by little. You learn a lot of things sitting in an exclusive pub after a round of golf. I discovered, for example, that I didn't need to be home in time for supper; I could arrive whenever I wanted, and a hot meal would still be waiting. I dipped my toes in slowly—a late night once a week—before it became two, three, then seven.

I also picked up whiskey, and realized that I enjoyed it better when she served it to me silently, without the constant chatter about couples therapy. Soon, I was raising my voice whenever she did, as if she were partially deaf and could only hear me when I was ten octaves louder.

My humble days as a mechanic thinned into the background and my courage grew fat on newfound wealth and power. I rented an apartment for a mistress, sometimes disappearing for weeks. She confronted me, of course—many times—but I'd brush her off with phrases I'd picked up in the pub. "Don't question me unless you're the one wearing the trousers in this house."

The night she poisoned my whiskey, I did not hear much besides shuffling feet and fading voices.

"Mom, I think I killed him."

"I thought you loved him?"

"I did, before he became a fool."

"Honey, you can put a monkey in a suit, but you can't buy it class." Were the final words I heard before darkness claimed me.

A Wedding Without A Groom

Mama Kibe moves slowly under the noonday sun. For a 60-year-old woman, she seems to have lived over a century. Her back is bent, and she walks with the aid of a mahogany hardwood stick, its handle lined with a golden bracelet. She moves with great effort towards her son, raises her hand—almost in slow motion—and traces his face with a wrinkled finger.

"Simon, you have come to cut the grass?"

"It's not Simon the gardener, Mom. It's your son, Kibe. Simon just left to take our bags to the servant quarters."

"Oh, my son, what a pleasant surprise. I was just about to have tea."

With labored breath, she turns to the figure standing next to her son.

"Njoki, what are you doing outside? You should be making tea."

"Mother, that is not Njoki, the maid. That is Winnie, my fiancée. You've met her a dozen times."

She rubs her eyes and looks at Winnie as if seeing her for the first time. "Forgive me, son, my memory is not what it used to be."

Winnie smiles painfully and turns her gaze from her.

With her back bent, Mama Kibe leads the way to the main house—a white, two-storey mansion with red roof tiles that dwarfs all the other houses around it. Kibe and Winnie follow, their steps muffled by the sound of her mahogany walking stick striking the pavement—clang, clang, clang, ding.

Son

KIBE WATCHES HIS mother disappear into the kitchen. *Where is the sugar? That's the salt.* He hears her muffled voice, and his face sags further. His mother had been vibrant. She was his father's right hand, helping him run his companies and excelling at it. But everything had changed after the car accident that claimed his father's life—a tragedy she had narrowly escaped. Now, she seemed to be wilting with every passing day.

Clang, clang, clang, ding. She enters the family room, leaning heavily on her walking stick. She turns, and with a heavy plop, collapses into her mocha brown leather recliner. The walking stick dangles by the recliner's left arm.

"You know, every day I can feel a part of me chip away, and I can tell I won't be around for long," she says in a voice that makes Kibe want to sob.

He had taken her to South Africa, India, and the United States, but the doctors found nothing. They attributed it to aging and fatigue from her years of hard work. *Which of their companies did her in?* Kibe wonders. *Was it the milk processing plant, the insurance firm, or the chain of supermarkets?*

"You're not going anywhere, Mother. You will live long enough to see your great-grandkids."

"Have you found someone? I want to know there will be someone to take care of you when I'm gone."

"Mother, I have a fiancée, Winnie." Kibe turns his gaze to her. "You've met her several times. You were at our *ruracio*."

Clang, clang, clang, ding. She gets up and traces a wrinkled finger around the face in front of her.

"Oh, wow. I must commend you, son, you made a brilliant choice; she is lovely."

"Mother, that's Njoki, the house girl, bringing tea. Winnie is right beside me."

Njoki sets down the tray, which holds a golden floral tea set, a teapot, three cups on saucers, a sugar dish, and three tiny spoons. She holds the sides of her blue maid's garb and curtsies before disappearing into the kitchen. Winnie tucks a long braid behind her ear and nervously taps her black low-heeled sandals on the hardwood floor. She smooths her long loose-fitting green dress and stares at a painting of Kibe as a child, wondering how anyone could confuse her with the maid.

While Njoki is in her early 20s, of average height and petite, with light brown skin, Winnie is in her late 20s, shorter, curvier, and with a darker complexion. Winnie's face is round, with small features, except for her big almond-shaped eyes. Their energies are also completely different—one gives off help and the other radiates lady of the manor. *How could she confuse us?* Winnie thinks, unsettled.

Clang, clang, clang, ding. Mama Kibe turns and, with a heavy plop, falls back into her leather recliner.

"Forgive me, son. My memory isn't what it used to be."

Fiancée

WINNIE TURNS HER gaze from the painting and glances at Mama Kibe, across from her. Dressed in a cream outfit—hat, coat, and blue pointed-toe flats with a golden chain—she exudes an outlandish, late-Queen-of-England look. *That couldn't be Njoki's doing; this is the work of a cultured mind that can see and coordinate colors*, Winnie thinks, as she raises to pour her a cup of tea. She drops two spoonfuls of sugar, stirs, and carefully hands her the cup.

She has never been in Mama Kibe's good books. It began after she moved into the servant's quarters next to the house with Kibe. Winnie didn't like how Kibe jumped to his mother's every beck and call: *Oh, Kibe, the sink is not working; the bulb needs changing; the groundskeeper is away and the compound is full of leaves.* She had convinced him to leave their Karen home to an apartment in Adams Arcade, which earned her a place on her mother-in-law's 'noisemakers' list.

Winnie pours a cup for herself and for her fiancé, Kibe, adding three spoonfuls of sugar in each before stirring and settling back on her seat. She also doesn't like how Mama Kibe runs the companies. Despite being a shareholder, Kibe isn't involved in the companies at all. The money passes through his mother before getting to his pocket.

"It's in the hands of lawyers, accountants, and professionals," his mother always says when Winnie urges him to probe further. This had moved her from the "noisemakers" list straight into the "black book."

"What did you put in the tea? It's sour." Mama Kibe raises her voice for the first time since they arrived.

Winnie holds her cup, confused.

"Yes, it's sour," Kibe adds, reaching for the sugar dish. "This is salt, not sugar," he says, inspecting it.

Mama Kibe leans forward. "It's my fault. I can no longer tell the difference between salt and sugar. Forgive me, my memory isn't what it used to be," she says, setting the teacup back on the tray and accidentally spilling some tea on her cream dress. She glances at Winnie.

"Maria, can you get the white napkins in the kitchen? Njoki must have forgotten them."

"It's Winnie," she replies, her tone edged with frustration.

Clang, clang, clang. Mama Kibe struggles to get up. "I'll just get them myself."

Winnie stays immobile for a moment. *If she wants to get them, let her. Mama Kibe and her bent back and her walking stick and her can't-tell-the-difference-between-salt-and-sugar memory. She will probably confuse bread for napkins,* Winnie thinks and a smile almost crosses her face.

"No, Mother, I'll get them," she hears herself say, standing quickly as Mama Kibe turns and, with a heavy plop, falls back into her leather recliner.

Son

KIBE WATCHES AS his mother grows restless.

"Maria, Maria! Did this girl go to get the napkins from another planet? At this rate, this will turn into a permanent stain."

Kibe shifts his weight in his seat, tired of constantly correcting her. Rubbing his palms on his black trousers, he wonders how to broach the subject weighing on his mind. He tugs at his green coat to adjust it—matching outfits had been Winnie's idea to show a unified front.

"We've set our wedding date for the first Saturday of next month," Kibe says abruptly, without preamble.

"Wedding?" Mama Kibe chokes, taken aback.

"Yes. We'll need money for the wedding planner, stylist, designer, and everything else."

"This wedding sounds like an extravagant affair."

Kibe stares at his black shoes. Winnie has a taste for extravagance, and it seems to grow by the day. Just yesterday, she increased the number of bridesmaids from four to eight, all to be dressed by a celebrity designer, and she added three more floors to the wedding cake. She's making changes on a whim, and Kibe is afraid of what she'll adjust next.

"We stay rich by making money, not by spending it," his mother says. "Besides, I am not in any condition to attend an event as grand as a wedding."

Kibe pauses, thinking. It's always the same story whenever he brings up the wedding. Winnie won't take another one of her planned dates getting pushed.

"We can take the vows here," he suggests. "That way, we'll cut down the costs, and you won't have to travel."

"You know my memory isn't what it used to be. Give me time to recuperate, or would you rob me of the gift of seeing my only child's wedding?"

Kibe changes gears. "What about the business? Don't you think it's time I got more involved?"

"You're a shareholder. You're the owner; that's as involved as it gets."

Kibe starts to respond, but his mother cuts him off.

"Let the lawyers, accountants, and professionals handle it while you enjoy it, eh, son?"

Clang, clang, clang, ding. She's getting up again. "Maria! Maria! Where did this girl go to fetch my napkins, or does the kitchen move when it sees her?"

Fiancée

WINNIE COMES BACK into the sitting room, and Mama Kibe turns her back and falls into her leather recliner with a plop.

"I am sorry to keep you waiting. This house is a maze, and Njoki is quite the chatterbox."

Winnie picks up a white napkin, kneels down, and moves to wipe the splotch on Mama Kibe's cream dress.

"Those are the wrong napkins," Mama Kibe barks. "What I need are beverages, not dinner napkins," she growls.

For someone who can't tell names apart or the difference between salt, and sugar, she sure knows her napkins. As Mama Kibe makes to get up, Winnie positions herself in such a way that she could knock the mahogany walking stick to the floor without anyone noticing.

If Mama Kibe falls, she will fall back into her recliner and Winnie can apologize. But Winnie is sure her survival instincts will kick in, and she will stand without the help of the walking stick, and Kibe can finally see her for the fraud she is.

Mama Kibe is now standing. Her left hand gropes for the walking stick, which is no longer there, and she topples onto the floor with a thud. Her cream dress covers her face as she shrieks again and again, "She wants to kill me!"

Mama Kibe

FROM HER BEDROOM upstairs, Mama Kibe can hear their argument in the family room.

"Jesus Christ, Winnie. Do you want to kill my mother?"

"She's faking it. FAKING IT!" Winnie barks.

"She is sick. As if memory loss and limping aren't bad enough, now you want her crippled?"

"She's controlling you."

"And you're not?"

"You can't see what's in front of you, Kibe. She's trying to hook you up with the maid."

"Jesus Christ, Winnie. She's my mother, not the devil."

"You just can't see it. She's pretending to be ill because she doesn't want you to marry me."

"Well, maybe I shouldn't!" Kibe barks.

Someone storms out, slamming the door.

Njoki enters Mama Kibe's bedroom, carrying a fresh cup of tea and a change of clothes.

"Can I ask you something?" she asks with a slight stammer.

"Go on, my daughter," Mama Kibe says.

"Why did you tell me to give her the wrong napkins and tell her you can walk without the walking stick?"

Mama Kibe gets out of bed and holds Njoki's face with both hands. "You'll understand soon, my daughter. And no more wearing maid clothes." She reaches into her drawer, pulling out a wad of cash. "Buy yourself some well-fitting dresses and show off those hips and that waist. It's time you started looking like you could be someone's wife, not someone's maid."

Mama Kibe changes into a lime green dress and coat, slips into her blue pointed-toe flats, picks up her walking stick from beside the bed, and goes to find her son.

Clang, clang, clang. Her walking stick dings.

Fiancée

Winnie paces back and forth in the servant quarters where they're staying during their visit, having cooled off a bit. "I have a family that loves me too, you know," she says, breathing fast. Kibe knows that all too well—a middle-class family that lives in Donholm, with a proud father and a reasonable mother who he's wished more than once could switch places with her mother.

"I have plenty of suitors," Winnie continues, and Kibe understands where her pride comes from. "My DMs are flooded, flooded! And I don't respond. All for you. And for what? For what? For this shame, this embarrassment?" She picks up her pace, her frustration growing.

"We will stay here for a few days so I can look after my mother," Kibe says, then immediately regrets it, realizing he should have waited until his fiancée cooled off completely.

"If you stay here, I am leaving," Winnie says, matter-of-factly.

"How dare you talk like that after almost crippling her? Is that what you want—for her to attend our wedding in a wheelchair?"

"What weeding?" Winnie mumbles.

"We will have a wedding, but my mother is prickly about the spending, so it might not be as expensive as you'd like it to be," Kibe says. "You might have to cut down on your bridesmaids, the tiers on the cake—all of it," he adds.

"It's always about your mother. Mother this, Mother that. I should have seen the signs. I should have known." Winnie sobs, picks up her phone, and dials for an Uber. After confirming, she grabs her suitcase and starts pulling her clothes from the closet. She begins packing her bathing suits; she had actually looked forward to swimming in their pool and sunbathing at the gazebo, but all those are dreams now.

She stuffs the long dresses and plain turtlenecks she'd brought to impress her mother-in-law, along with her Bata Ngoma rubber shoes, into the suitcase without much order. Her phone dings, notifying her that her Uber has arrived, and she rolls the suitcase out of the servant quarters.

"Come back here! I am talking to you, Winnie," Kibe calls, following her outside. The moon is a white ball in the sky, and with the outdoor lights, the compound almost looks like day. Simon, who also doubles as their watchman, is still around. Kibe glances at him and wonders how his mother would confuse them. While he is tall, slender, and in his 30s, Simon is built like a tree trunk with a square jaw and broad shoulders, looking to be in his 40s.

"You can marry your mother—or that maid she's pushing you toward," Winnie snaps as she opens the door to a purple Toyota Passo, jolting Kibe out of his thoughts.

"You don't mean that," he says.

"Oh, but I do," Winnie replies, entering the Passo and slamming the door as the driver puts her suitcase in the boot and gets back into the car.

"Open this door," Kibe barks while reaching for the handle that won't budge. Winnie's arms are folded in the backseat, and she seems to be contemplating her decision.

Clang, clang, clang. Mama Kibe's walking stick dings. "Let her cool off, son; she will be back," she says warmly, removing her son's fingers from the Passo's door handle. Immediately she does, Winnie gives the driver directions to her family's house in Donholm, and the car speeds out of the compound. "You look exhausted; go and lie down in the servant quarters, and I'll call you when supper is ready," Mama Kibe adds.

Arrangements

Kibe's mind is dizzy as he returns to the servant quarters; it's as if a bee is buzzing in one ear and out of the other. He picks up his phone and dials Winnie again. The call goes straight to voicemail. *Come back, and let's work this out.* He texts, adding to the string of unanswered messages he has already sent.

He drops his phone on the coffee table, sinks into the couch, and scrolls through channels on an old Sony TV with a fat back. Gray vertical streaks resembling rain fill the screen most of the time. *When it rains, it pours,* Kibe thinks as sleep from exhaustion takes him.

"Mr. Kibe, Mr. Kibe, are you asleep?" He's woken up by a soft voice.

"Winnie, you came back," he says drowsily. "I knew you would, babe," he adds. Rubbing his eyes, he realizes the figure in front of him—with freshly braided hair, a slim fitting black dress that cuts above the knee, and black ankle-strap shoes, holding a tray of food—is not his fiancée.

"Who are you?" he stammers.

"It's Njoki; your mother sent me," she says, smiling.

"Njoki?" Kibe says in disbelief. "You look like a completely different person—in a good way," he adds quickly after noticing the confusion on her face.

"I brought your supper," Njoki says, placing the tray on the table.

"Thank you, Njoki," Kibe says, opening the plate cover to find his favorite dish—chicken fried with red and green peppers, rice, and avocado salad. He takes a bite, savoring the flavors that burst in his mouth. "You cooked this?" he asks the shy Njoki, who is standing with her face to the floor.

"Yes, I did," she chirps.

"It's really good," Kibe says. "Don't worry, I'll bring the dishes after I'm done." He glances at her as she leaves, still in disbelief that she's the same person.

Kibe removes his green coat and finishes his meal, then picks up his phone to call Winnie again. He finds her voicemail and leaves another message before resting his head on the couch arm, drifting back to sleep.

The following morning, the same soft voice wakes him. This time, Njoki wears a pink dress, even shorter than the previous one, paired with pink block heels. She's carrying a tray with mango juice, sausages, eggs, bacon, and bread. Kibe takes the food and dismisses her, still feeling grumpy from all the calls and messages he has left Winnie that remain unanswered.

Before noon, Njoki appears with cleaning supplies, wearing a short black-and-white maids dress that reveals yellow collarbones and thighs. She spends her time in the servant quarters, bending to wipe the floor and kneeling to reach corners. Kibe finds himself glancing away from his phone and the rain-streaked TV, toward the tableau that Njoki is painting.

"Where did you go to school?" He finds himself asking, sparking a conversation that moves from her schooling to where she grew up, her parents' passing, and how her brother raised her, and eventually to relationships.

At noon, Njoki brings Kibe his lunch, still dressed in her maid's attire; *ugali*, fried meat and *sukuma*. Instead of dismissing her, Kibe uses one of the plate covers to share a portion of his food with her. "This is for you," he says, matter-of-factly. Njoki sits next to him, and they eat together, talking about everything and nothing, laughing until their plates are empty. She gathers the dishes, and as she leaves, Kibe catches himself seeing her for the first time—not as a maid but as a woman.

In the evening, Njoki reappears in a red tennis skirt, a white top that reveals her cleavage, and white Bata Ngomas, carrying two plates, two spoons and three hotpots on a tray: one with chicken stew, another with *chapati*, and the third with salad. That evening, no conversation fills the air; only the sound of eating and another, more primal sound as Njoki stays in the servants' quarters with Kibe for the night.

Mama Kibe

Clang, clang, clang, ding. Mama Kibe walks into the living room where her son waits. She wears a forest green dress suit, a matching hat, a pearl necklace, and white shoes. A month has come and gone, and this is their first proper sit-down since Kibe started seeing Njoki.

Kibe is dressed in a brown shirt, black trousers, and blue slippers. He knows she is aware of his involvement with Njoki, but he doesn't know what to expect from her. Over the years, he has learned the capriciousness of her mother— sometimes scolding him for triumphs and congratulating him for what he considers failures.

Kibe watches his mother walk to her recliner, noticing that her limp isn't as bad as it was when Winnie was around. He had thought it would worsen after her fall, yet somehow it seems to have improved. He watches her plop down on the sofa and lean her walking stick against the arm of the chair.

"Good morning, Mother," Kibe says. "How are you feeling today?"

"Much better," Mama Kibe says. "The devil tries you, but God always prevails." Clang, clang, clang, ding. She stamps her walking stick on the floor before leaning it back on the arm of the chair. "Amen," she adds after a moment's silence.

"Amen," Kibe echoes, not entirely sure what he's agreeing to. Just then, Njoki enters with tea. She is provocatively dressed in an orange dress despite the cold morning, with black strapped heels and a freshly styled ponytail. Kibe looks at her without meeting her gaze. *He should be more careful with her,* he thinks. *He should be using protection, even when she insists that she's on her 'safe days'.*

Kibe swallows the lump in his throat. He should have gone to get Winnie from her parents' house, but his mother kept coming up with excuses not to accompany him. He should have gone alone, yet the guilt of his infidelity eats him from the inside out, leaving him unsure of how to face her.

Njoki sets the ivory-colored, rose-patterned teapot, cups, sugar dish, and silver spoons on the table. She pours each of them a cup, stirs two spoonfuls of sugar in Mama Kibe's cup and three in Kibe's, then curtsies and disappears back to the kitchen.

"What do you think of Njoki?" Mama Kibe asks after taking a sip of tea.

"She has really transformed," Kibe replies, avoiding his mother's gaze.

"She's told me you can't seem to get enough of her and admitted she can't get enough of you either."

Kibe stares at his cup of tea, realizing for the first time the appeal of Njoki to his mother. Njoki would follow Mama Kibe's instructions without question, acting as her eyes and ears, sharing every detail of his life.

"She'd make a good wife," Mama Kibe remarks. "She won't be confusing your sugar with salt," she adds, taking another sip of tea.

Kibe realizes he needs to speak up before things get out of hand. "Mom, you know I still plan on marrying Winnie, don't you?" he says. "Njoki is a good distraction, but eventually, I'll have to get back to the life I'm building for myself."

Mama Kibe's jaw tightens briefly. "How can you go back to a woman who doesn't even pick your calls or respond to your messages? You should let that ship sail and look ahead." She glances at Njoki, who enters the room to ask if they need anything else. Mama Kibe signals they don't, and Njoki curtsies and leaves.

"I know Winnie; she'll come around," Kibe says, having had enough of the conversation. He gets up and heads to his quarters, knowing that, despite deciding to move forward with Winnie, Njoki will bring his supper, and they will likely spend another night together.

Mama Kibe leans back in her recliner, lost in thought. She realizes it was naive to think her son would move on from his fiancée so quickly. Winnie's parents are coming on the morrow to resolve things, and Mama Kibe had hoped Kibe would be done with Winnie by now. She smiles realizing the in-laws coming presents the perfect opportunity for her to rid her son off his fiancée once and for all.

In-laws

WINNIE'S DAD PUTS his 2007 Toyota Corolla in park on Mama Kibe's compound at exactly 11:00 a.m., and gets out. He is in a brown Kaunda suit, a Casio watch, and black leather shoes that have been polished to the point they catch the sun and gleam. Despite being close in age to Mama Kibe, he still has the handsomeness of his youth and his gait has been unaffected by old age.

He walks to the passenger seat and opens the door for Mama Winnie, a plump, kind-hearted woman in her 50s who is in a brown and green *kitenge* dress with green plaid pumps. She's carrying a Naivas bag full of groceries—sugar, maize flour, cooking oil—enough food to last Mama Kibe's household a month. They know Mama Kibe doesn't need it, but they are people who believe in courtesy.

Winnie's door is the last one to open. She's wearing a long, dark gray, shapeless frock that covers her arms and feet. Initially, she'd chosen jeans and a crop top that revealed her belly button piercing. Her arms were also bare, revealing her rose tattoo. She had decided if she was going to marry into the family, it was time she became herself. A deeper part of her also wanted to rub it into Mama Kibe's face.

Her mother had taken one look at her and dragged her by the arm back to her bedroom. "Do you want to embarrass us?" she'd scolded. "We're going to your in-laws, not a club on Ngong Road." She'd then reached into the darkest corners of Winnie's closet and pulled out this rarely worn dress.

Clang, clang, clang, ding. Mama Kibe greets them at the door and welcomes them in. She's in a lilac dress and coat, yellow shoes, and hat. Her mouth smiles, but her eyes don't. "Nungira, come and take this shopping to the kitchen," she calls out. Winnie notices the new house girl—a slender girl who looks to be in her late teens. She is quick on her feet and with none of the looks Njoki had. She breathes out a sigh, feeling a bit secure of her position in the home.

Mama Kibe sits on her recliner as Nungira brings tea in a cream teapot set adorned with pink lilies. She glances at Winnie and immediately looks away. "Thank you for visiting me," Mama Kibe says. "I am an old woman, and every bit of company helps."

"It's the least we could do," Baba Winnie says warmly. "You have a beautiful home; I'm always impressed when I come here."

"This old, empty thing?" Mama Kibe sighs. "I have done my best, but there's only so much an old woman can do." She tries to appeal to Baba Winnie's ego. *In another life, they might have become a couple,* she thinks, *and she would have pushed him to become something more than a regular high school principal.*

"It's not empty," Baba Winnie says amiably. "You've got your son and Winnie, and soon it will be filled with grandchildren."

"Amen," Mama Winnie adds.

"Amen," Winnie whispers.

"Amen," Mama Kibe echoes with another half-smile.

Winnie stands to pour everyone a cup of tea, double-checking the sugar before dropping two spoonful's in every cup, except hers, which she drops three spoonful's and stirs.

They drink in silence, with only slurping sounds being heard. After a while, Winnie gets uncomfortable and shifts her weight from side to side to get comfortable before eyeing her dad.

"Speaking of unions and children, where is your son? I'd hoped he would be here with us so we could resolve this small problem together."

"Kibe has been greatly affected by all this. He swears he never wants to see Winnie again, but I know those are words spoken in the heat of the moment," Mama Kibe says. "He's just as hot-headed as his father was. The moment he sees Winnie, I'm sure he'll change his mind."

Winnie stares at the wall, thinking how odd it is that Kibe won't stop blowing up her phone, yet he supposedly doesn't want to see her.

"Let's finish our tea and find him in the servant quarters. It's not as big as this house, but my husband built it to fit a family of five," Mama Kibe mentions, hinting that her quarters are grander than Baba Winnie's Donholm house.

Clang, clang, clang, ding. Mama Kibe reaches the servant quarters door with her in-laws following close behind. "Kibe, Kibe, Kibe," she calls, but no one responds; there is loud music playing inside. "Kids these days," she says, shrugging at her uneasy in-laws before pushing the door open.

What they see makes Baba Winnie turn around, grab her wife's and daughter's hands, and head for his Toyota Corolla. Kibe, dazed, remains frozen in place—he's on the couch, naked, on top of Njoki wondering if those were his in-laws or shadows. When he finally registers what just happened, he gets off Njoki, wears a gray bathrobe and runs barefoot to the parking lot but by then, the white Toyota Corolla has vanished, and Simon is closing the gate.

Kibe heads back inside, grabs his phone, and tries to call Winnie, only to find he's been blocked.

The Wedding

Kibe starts zoning out around the third month since his in-laws visited. He can barely hear anything now except the faint sounds of his mother's walking stick approaching, followed by her familiar voice, though the words are mostly lost on him, he nods automatically. He's unsure how he reached this point—maybe it was after going to Winnie's to apologize, only for her to chase him away, or seeing her later on Instagram enjoying baecations with another man.

Mama Kibe's voice cuts through his daze. She says something about Njoki and vomiting, and from what he can make out, something about avoiding children born out of wedlock. The wedding must be held, and quickly, before Njoki starts showing. Kibe stares blankly at his own portrait on the wall, nodding in agreement.

In the next couple of days, the mansion becomes a beehive of activity. No cost is spared as tailors parade in and out, measuring outfits for the bride, groom, bridesmaid, and groomsmen. Chefs arrive with cake samples and elaborate cuisines. Kibe half-registers a voice asking, "How does that taste?" though he can't recall taking the bite he's chewing. He nods absentmindedly, and someone thanks him.

Clang, clang, clang, ding. He hears the faint taps of his mother's walking stick and the soft sound of her settling into her recliner. "The mansion's grounds are too small for the wedding," she says. "We'll hold it in one of the ballrooms at Windsor Country Club. I want Njoki to arrive in a horse-drawn carriage and, afterward, you'll both leave in a helicopter." Kibe mutters something, which makes his mother's face tighten.

"I know I said we stay rich by not spending money, but this is your wedding; it only happens once." Kibe murmurs another response, prompting a sharper reaction from her.

"What do you mean it sounds like it's my wedding? Kibe, I didn't raise you to talk back to your elders. The wedding is tomorrow. Bring a better attitude, if not for me, then for your wife, Njoki."

GUESTS START POURING into Windsor from 10:00 a.m.—esteemed friends made through years of empire-building, the Minister of Trade, the Governor of Nairobi, and upper management from their various organizations.

A musician from Lagos serenades the guests with gentle tunes as Mama Kibe arrives in a black Cadillac Escalade, looking resplendent in a silver gown with gold ornaments. She wears it in such a way that if you saw her before seeing the bride, you would think the occasion was hers. She leans on a blue walking stick with a golden handle. Clang, clang, clang, ding. She waves to some of the guests before taking her seat.

Soon, two black limousines pull up, and twelve groomsmen in blue suits step out, followed by Kibe. He's dressed sharply in a three-piece blue suit with gold embroidery, a short-tailed coat cut at the front with golden lapels, matching waistcoat, cravat, and blue velvet shoes. He looks dapper and even appears to be in a good mood.

"Excuse me, I need to use the washrooms," he hears himself say to his groomsmen as they settle into their seats. As he does, two white limousines arrive, and twelve bridesmaids in gold satin dresses, with a slit on the right that starts at their gold pumps and stops above their knees, step out, each holding a small bouquet of blue roses. A blue Porsche Cayenne follows, and out-steps the maid of honor and best man. The maid of honor's dress is also gold but it's embroidered with blue roses along the waistline, while the best man wears a blue suit with gold lapels.

The bride arrives last in a cream carriage drawn by a white destrier. Njoki is breathtaking in a milk-white ball gown that is form fitting on her chest then spills over like boiling milk from her waist to the floor, complemented by a golden tiara, necklace, and bracelets.

She sits next to her brother, who's elegantly dressed in a black suit. As they prepare to step out of the carriage, one of the security detail stops them, and another whispers to Mama Kibe that Kibe is nowhere to be found. His groomsmen say he went to the washrooms, but he has not been found in any of them.

Njoki is directed to a hotel room with her maid of honor as Mama Kibe steps outside to make a call. Irritated, she calls Kibe's number, but like everyone else who has tried, she hears only the automated message, "The person you are calling is not reachable."

Desperate, she sends people to her house in Karen and their apartment in Adams Arcade. "Break in if you must. Bring him here by any means necessary," she orders. Clang, clang, clang, ding. She returns to the head table, exchanging polite greetings with familiar faces, though her agitation is barely contained.

Half an hour later, her phone buzzes. Both properties are empty, with no sign of Kibe. Mama Kibe tries calling him again and again and gets the same message. In her frustration, she leaves a string of furious messages.

"Come here right this moment."

"I won't forgive you for this."

"You are with that skunk Winnie, aren't you?"

She sends her security detail to Winnie's house, but soon learns that her parents are oblivious about any wedding, and Winnie is ziplining at Kereita Forest with her new boyfriend.

"Don't embarrass me like this."

"Please, come."

"I'm begging you."

She resorts to pleading, but Kibe remains unresponsive.

By 3:00 p.m., the guests have grown restless and they are whispering among themselves. Mama Kibe is aware that word has gotten round that the groom is a no-show. She speaks to the master of ceremony, who directs the wait staff to begin serving food.

As the sun dips lower, the guests have eaten their fill, some preparing to leave, and Kibe is still nowhere to be found. "You know how kids can be sometimes," Mama Kibe mutters to the Governor and Minister of Trade as she shakes their hands and thanks them, with the color of embarrassment painted all over her face. *He will hear from me when I see him,* she consoles herself.

Yet Kibe does not appear—not that evening, the next day, or the next month. A private security firm is hired to search for him around the world, but month after month, they come back empty handed. Short of Kibe and short of any information on his whereabouts.

Clang, clang, clang, ding. Mama Kibe's walking stick can be heard through the quiet mansion in Karen. Njoki remains by her side, caring for her, as her young daughter plays around the house. But Mama Kibe seldom speaks. Lost in thought, she sits in her recliner, wondering where her son disappeared to.

Imperfect Match

Debra

Let me tell you how high the stakes can get; when your life is tied to another person tightly enough, they are sky-high. Friends, family, a concerned neighbor, even a stranger on the road might be quick to tell you to leave, but what do they know about high stakes? Or about love so intoxicating it makes doing the most heinous things feel normal?

What do they know about that kind of love when their own connections are flimsy? A text here, another there. Sex. Ghosting. And they repeat the cycle. Even the ones who have a connection find that time has made it threadbare. Their relationships have become purely functional—bills, errands, school functions, family gatherings. The humdrum of it all, to the point that they sleep in the same bed like siblings. So, of course, their immediate advice is for you to leave because they are on the verge of leaving whatever it is they have themselves.

Leaving has never been an option for me, even after one person after another told me to. I have always known I would never leave. I have worn every hat. I have played the jealous girlfriend, the detective who follows her boyfriend around, and now, the woman with a gun pointed at my best friend, ready to pull the trigger and play a murderer.

How did we get here? You see, I was like you. I wanted something normal too. A decent man. Preferably with a head on his shoulders, who believed in the equality of the sexes, and had a steady income. It didn't have to be anything extravagant, but not underwhelming to the point where he had to excuse himself to the bathroom every time a bill showed up. That's not too much for a 27-year-old girl to ask for, is it?

We would have a kid or two, and in time, our connection would fade. Like everyone else, our relationship would revolve around bills, errands, school functions, family gatherings—the humdrum of life. And if at any point down the road I discovered something about him I couldn't live with, I could simply take the advice of family, friends, a concerned neighbor, or even a stranger on the road, and leave.

I got exactly what I was looking for in Joshua—well, somewhat. What is a well-rounded human woman if not for compromise? Joshua was around 5'10", dark brown, and masculine with broad shoulders. Our romance started like most workplace romances—noticing him in meetings, realizing I liked how he dressed, talked, and carried himself, stealing glances. Him giving me the, 'What time does that skirt suit and those panties come off?' eyes and me returning the favor in kind and giving him the, 'Anytime for you' eyes. Introductions followed. Turns out he was consulting for our beverage company and soon enough, my panties were off and he was consulting for my flora and fauna too.

I fell for him hard, and within no time, I was leaving my project management job and moving to his four-bedroom bungalow in Loresho as a full-time girlfriend. A welcome change from my one-bedroom flat in Embakasi. For the first time in years, I wouldn't have to hear quarreling neighbors or endure their unwelcome, obscene loud moans at night and weekends. The loudest sounds in this part of town were birds singing, the occasional cough of our gardener's lawnmower, and the barking of German Shepherds and Golden Retrievers while I lounged on the pool deck, sunbathing and reading my book. Nothing that couldn't be fixed by stepping inside the house and closing the heavy mahogany doors behind me.

In Loresho, I had a different set of problems. I rubbed shoulders with people who used words like 'scarlet' and 'crimson' instead of just saying 'red'. They had brunch and flew out as casually as I used to take *matatus*—that was before Joshua bought me a crimson Mazda CX-5. I'm a quick study. See how quickly I added the lingo into my vocabulary?

Anything for the great love of my life, who was spoiling me rotten with affection, date nights, and all the sex I could ask for. Normal things in a romance, right? Wrong. After the initial excitement of our relationship wore off—I think it was around the eight-month mark—he began using those things as rewards for my good behavior and withholding them whenever I 'misbehaved.'

Of course, good and bad behavior were up to his discretion, and soon, I became an addict—suffering withdrawal symptoms whenever I didn't get my fix. I would become sullen when I had displeased him and my pulse would quicken, and my breath would shorten when I knew I had pleased him and like a good puppy, it was time to be rewarded with a treat. Little did I know that this would open a can of worms that would ultimately turn me into a murderer.

But let's set murder aside and look back at the girl who wanted ordinary things—a man who doesn't let a day go by without checking on you, a man who takes you out every other weekend and makes you feel special. Good sex. Plans for the future with you in them. He sensed how deeply I was tied to these things and began using them bit by bit. I didn't notice at first, and when I did, it was too late.

The first time it happened, I had called him. He sounded distracted, and I wanted his full attention, so I told him to call me back when he was less preoccupied. He never did, and I ended up calling to ask why he hadn't gotten back to me. He casually said he had meant to but didn't see the issue since I'd called back anyway.

Do you see how a girl can feel gaslighted? After that, I learned to say what I needed to, whether he was present or distracted. He was often inattentive and when he sounded engaged, it was usually after I'd done something for him—like the blowjobs I hated giving or the laundry and cooking I resented doing. Whenever he sounded distant, I found myself wondering if I'd failed at one of these tasks.

Lucy

I CALLED MY best friend, Lucy. We met way back in campus, and the one thing I loved about her was her free spirit. She was willing to try almost anything at a moment's notice. I asked her to join me for a lunch date. Money has never been a problem for us. Joshua, an Electrical Engineer by profession, is remarkable at his job. He invented an automatic thermostat for bathrooms, and as long as it is in stores, he cashes checks—it happens to be available in 43 countries, the same age he'll be turning next year.

He has set up an office as a full-time consultant in Upper Hill, though he doesn't need to be there. He has never been selfish with his money where I am concerned. God knows, like that thermostat, he controls me in other ways.

Lucy and I met at Artcaffé in Westgate Mall. The January sun was high in the sky. I was in a purple Valentino sequin midi dress and green Louboutins. I remember Lucy whistling when she saw me—a habit she picked up after I started seeing Joshua and overhauled my wardrobe. She was in a white t-shirt, masterfully knotted to reveal her belly button and piercing, paired with blue jeans folded at the bottom and white sneakers, something from Mr. Price or LC Waikiki. While I looked elegant, she looked hot, and for a split second, I wanted to trade places with her.

After teasing me with every *mubaba* rhetoric she could muster, Lucy ordered a burger, and I had linguine carbonara—something else I picked from my affluent neighbors. I shared my concerns about the great love of my life. Her advice was simple: I should leave. Leave and go where? I had wanted to ask her. My mistake for seeking advice from someone who was ever on Tinder.

You could go mad with all that sexual selection—running through people, unsure if you left the right one behind, or if they were ahead or somewhere in the middle. As we went through her prospects, I started feeling dizzy. Sometimes, I think Tinder was just her way of adding excitement into her life with the mundane melodrama of different sexual partners, not to get into something serious. *All those prospects? Pick one already. I mean, come on, Lucy.*

This only reinforced my commitment to Joshua. I got used to the blowjobs, the cooking, and the laundry, but he wanted it done a certain way and started using other methods to control me. Like saying 'thank you' after I was done taking him in my mouth, then getting up, having a shower, and going to bed when my whole body was pining to have him inside me.

I would ask him what was wrong, and he would say nothing, and I would be the one going through my mind, trying to figure out if I had done something that had displeased him. Had I used my teeth on him? Was the food too salty? Or were his clothes not pressed enough?

You might be thinking that doing all those chores was not worth being ignored. But for a speck of his attention, it was. When he was present, I was in heaven. The conversations flowed. We talked for hours about everything, from childhood, to teenage years to adulthood. We shared stories about how her mother left him, how his uncle, who is now abroad, took him in and educated him, how both of my parents passed away from old age, and about my stepbrother, whom I haven't seen in years.

When we were not reminiscing, we were doing chores together, which oftentimes turned to steamy sex. It was for those very moments that I labored so hard. But now the icy days were here and they did not seem to be leaving.

I was looking to bring them to a brisk end. I bought new lingerie from Bluebella and changed my hairstyle from sister-locks to braids that touched the small of my back. I could have bought Fenty, but Joshua worshiped at the altar of natural beauty, which I was lucky to have with my honey mustard complexion and a face that made men and women stare. I could have gone to the gym, too, if it weren't for my hourglass figure that never changes, regardless of what I eat.

All the same, Joshua remained stoic, coming home from work, having his meal, taking a shower, wearing his dark blue pajamas, and sitting in bed with a book. "Put the book away," I said one evening, clad in my sensual black sheer Bluebella lingerie while biting on a strawberry. You guessed it—I had brought fruits to the bedroom; what are the chances I was Eve, and like Adam, he would take a bite?

"I am tired. Some other time," he said without removing his gaze from his book. He was reading *The Count of Monte Cristo* by Alexandre Dumas. I had picked up the book but couldn't get past the third page. I preferred electrifying authors like Sidney Sheldon, Gillian Flynn, and Danielle Steel. Novels that actually went somewhere.

Left in the cold for a dull book, I felt the punch in my gut as I put the strawberries away, covered myself with a white sateen bed sheet that hugged me like a second skin, supported myself with two of the six gray pillows on the king-size bed, and picked up *Tell Me Your Dreams* by Sidney Sheldon. He glanced at me momentarily. "It's funny how all books have a spine when most stories are spineless," he said before getting back to *Monte Cristo*. In a strange way, I felt as if the jab was directed to me and my choices.

You would think all these things would make me ambivalent toward him, but my attraction was swollen to bursting, and my resolve was full to overflowing. I became more devious and creative. I called Lucy on Valentine's day and managed to convince her to share our bed. They say every girl has fantasies of being with another girl, and it just so happened that Lucy was having an experimental phase.

It didn't hurt that Lucy had a sultriness about her that I could never pull off. With her dark chocolate complexion, petite frame, average height, short hair, and the ability to make any piece of clothing that she wore look enchanting. She was the kind of woman who men described as having sex appeal, a compliment that was far and in-between in my life.

Joshua welcomed it with open arms. Not even Dumas could make him turn down this once-in-a-lifetime opportunity. I mean, it's every guy's dream—a threesome with his girlfriend's friend. And it worked. For the next three months, I was given queen treatment. That was before he wanted to do it again, but Lucy was no longer up for it because she had gotten a steady boyfriend. I suppose Tinder does work after all.

That was when things started going downhill. Everything was rationed: the calls, my time with him, and the sex faded altogether. Now, a sane person would tell me to look elsewhere, and that was what everybody said—a concerned neighbor, a stranger on the road, and even good old Lucy and her Tinder partner. But how could I look elsewhere when every man I looked at had Joshua's face? His DNA was imprinted on me. I would either have him or go mad trying to get him.

I decided to do some detective work after realizing that his coldness might have been brought by warmth from another woman. I figured I might as well put Sidney Sheldon's detective chapters to good use. I found myself in Gikomba market buying a black coat, a cap, and sunglasses. Gikomba felt like a good bet because there are no paper trails.

Later, I found myself leaving my Mazda CX-5 behind and commuting to a second-hand car lot to hire a Suzuki Swift. *Nothing to see here, just another Uber driver trying to make a living.* I thought. There was a paper trail in that. Sidney Sheldon didn't cover this part, and as you can see, I was an amateur in this, clutching at straws.

I trailed him, behind the windshield of the Suzuki Swift. Joshua was all work, then drinks with a few friends, and then back home to me. It warmed my heart and convinced me that truly, there was something I wasn't doing. The *chapos* got softer, the house cleaner and the clothes were so sharply ironed they could cut tomatoes, but he was still distant.

I found myself opening a Tinder account and using an alias to try to get us another threesome. I quickly realized he wouldn't like any of the girls who matched with me; they were made up, with acres of tattoos, caked faces, and fluttering eyelashes. It was strange that they were looking for something real when they appeared so fake. I deleted my account upon realizing that inviting one over might make him even more distant.

If he was not getting any elsewhere, that was okay. I decided to buy a dildo and play with myself instead, while I waited for time to pass; they do say that time is the best healer and the best teacher. Time was a lot of things, but it was not the best lover. With my new dildo in my right hand and my phone in my left with Joshua's picture, the sensation felt nothing to what he felt like on those days when he made love to me.

Time slowly but surely helped. I had fallen into a routine, and we were gradually becoming one of those couples with flimsy connections. Making his breakfast in the morning, making the bed, tidying up the house, cooking his meals, and taking a shower before sitting down with a novel to wait for him. When he came home, our conversations mostly consisted of the words 'yes' and 'no.'

I think he sensed I was drifting off because he checked in out of the blues at lunchtime. "Dress up, Debra. I want to take you somewhere," he said and I was hurriedly having a shower, putting on my Fendi ruched sand-brown dress and heels and we were off to the movies at Imax, Sarit Center. Seated at the back, giggling like high school students while I struggled to watch the movie because he was busy finger fucking me and God knows I needed it.

We left the theater halfway through the movie, and it was then that I remembered that I had left my coat back at home, and there was Joshua, a perfect gentleman covering me up with his black Brioni Jacket. Not that it covered me for long. It was soon off me as he took me in his Mercedes at the basement parking lot and later finished me off at the house.

"Aren't you going back to work?" I asked him.

"I took the afternoon off. Today is all about you, Debs," he responded. Sometimes he used the nickname to make me feel special, but other times it reminded me of my Geography teacher saying, "*Empty debes make the worst noise.*"

I shrugged off the memory, happy to have him all to myself again. We cuddled on the couch, savoring each other's company, talking, laughing, gossiping, laughing some more and making future plans. When I got up to prepare supper, he gently stopped me and ordered takeout instead, letting us continue basking in the magic of the moment.

The next morning, I threw away my dildo and got into my CX-5 to drive to the Carrefour at Sarit Center to buy fresh supplies for the house. Besides shopping, I also wanted to relieve the euphoria of my date with Joshua from the previous day. As I entered the mall, I saw them: Lucy and Joshua, hand in hand, riding up the escalator, and disappearing out of sight. This is where I was meant to leave, but instead, I found myself online, searching for a black market gun.

Gunslinger

I WAS IN a dark *buibui* and equally dark sunglasses as I approached the Airbnb in South C where the seller had told me to meet him. It was a cold July morning, but I barely noticed the chill. My heart raced, my armpits were damp, and my palms sweaty. *What if he is an undercover cop? Or worse, a predator?* The thought made me want to turn back.

But the image of Lucy in Joshua's arms fueled my resolve to move forward.

I joined Kawi Complex Road in my hired Suzuki Swift, and remembered how I had gotten a hold of this faceless black-hat I was on my way to meet. On a message board on the internet. You didn't get his number—you left yours, and after he had done some digging he would decide if you were worth calling. Now, here I was, unsure if I had been deemed worthy or just vulnerable.

I stopped at the gate of Parkview Apartments, told the guard the apartment I was going to and he allowed me in. *A witness? An accomplice? Or someone who was just doing their job?* I wondered as I parked my car in the extensive compound and got out. There were kids riding bikes outside—*A good omen,* I thought as I climbed up the stairs to the second floor of Parkview Apartments, my right hand clutching to the taser in my handbag that I had bought as an afterthought, and knocked on the door to apartment 19.

After what felt like five minutes, the door cracked open slightly before swinging fully ajar. The man in front of me didn't look like a gun seller, but then again, I didn't look like a murderer either. He was tall and athletic, wearing an avocado-green cap, a white polo shirt, khakis, and dark brown boots. His brows, beard, complexion, and demeanor suggested he was either Arabian or from the North Eastern part of Kenya.

"My name is Aisha," I heard myself lie.

"Come in, Aisha," he said without introducing himself.

I walked into the living room, which was modernly furnished with graying fabric sofas, and a large flat-screen TV—typical of most Airbnb's in the city. The gun seller moved to the sofa where a black backpack lay. I studied him further; he didn't look like a criminal. He carried himself like someone who had once lived an upright life but had been dealt a bad hand and was now doing what he had to do to survive.

"What's your name?" I stammered.

"No need for that," he said, breaking the handle of the *jembe* that had begun digging his backyard.

He rummaged through the backpack and pulled out a silver gun with a brown handle. The gravity of the weapon made me take two steps back. "This is a Smith & Wesson .38 revolver. It holds five bullets. The serial numbers have been filed off, which means it's untraceable. It also means that you don't want the police catching you with it," he began, without preamble, as he handed me the weapon.

It felt heavy on my hand, and it didn't help that I was trembling like a leaf. "You'll need to fire a couple of rounds before you can use it," he said. "I'd suggest Ngong Hills—it's nice and secluded, with no paper trails," he added.

After showing me how to use it, I gave him 130,000 Kenya shillings and took the Wesson together with 10 bullets in a box and stuffed them in my handbag. "I am a ghost if the government catches up with you but I'm always available if you need to do business," he said as I left the Airbnb and headed towards Ngong Hills.

Ngong Hills was shrouded in mist, and for the first time, my bones felt the bite of the cold. It didn't help that my Suzuki Swift lacked both a heater and air conditioning. I drove deeper into the hills. The area was largely deserted, but I knew lovers sometimes came here for picnics, so I was careful. I turned on my headlights and swept the area before getting out of the car.

I fired the first round. It was louder than I expected. I waited to see if someone would show, but no one did. The lovers must have thought it was fireworks, the soundtrack to their undying love. And with the July cold, they must have been perched close-knit and tightly together, too distracted to care about my antics.

The shot had made my arm vibrate to the point I missed my mark, which was the center of a big circle I had drawn with my red lipstick on a tree. The second shot missed the mark too, so did the third and fourth, but the fifth one landed right in the circle, and the sixth one was spot on. I decided to fire a seventh for good measure. After all, I only needed one bullet to get the job done.

It was like most Sundays. Joshua was seated on one of the purple velvet sofas by the fireplace in his blue pajamas, distant as usual. I think he was reading *Desperate Characters* by Paula

Fox. Another tedious book. If he had been consistent with his affection, I might have let the affair slide. But how could I let it slide now, knowing he wasn't fully present because he was philandering with my best friend? *Kikulacho ki nguoni mwako,* I thought painfully.

"Guess who is visiting for lunch?" I said knowingly. Despite the cold season I was in a yellow sundress, brown fluffy slippers, and my hair was freshly braided. In my heart of hearts, I hoped I would catch his eye and all this madness would come to an end.

"Who?" he asked irritably, without taking his eyes off his book. His tone was filled with boredom because that's all I had become to him—a bore.

"Lucy," I said.

"Oh, is that right?" He closed his book momentarily and looked at me for the first time in a while. He tried to maintain the boredom in his voice, but I could feel the glee and excitement underneath.

Lucy showed up brimming with energy. Joshua put his book away and looked at her as if she were otherworldly. She wore a maroon puffer jacket, white sports bra, maroon leggings, black Timberlands, and on her hands a brown hobo bag. I kept wondering what sorcery she was using to make that outfit work, as she went on and on about how her Tinder relationship was blossoming and how love comes from the most unexpected places.

I felt the .38 revolver in my waistband press against my hip bone every time I glanced at Joshua. He was staring unashamedly, his mouth slightly open—the only thing missing was drool. Every time Lucy put the words 'love,' 'Tinder,' and 'blossom' in the same sentence, it became harder to bear. When I couldn't take it anymore, I pulled out the Wesson. My hand was shaking. I should have practiced in front of people instead of trees.

"The nerve of you, going behind my back and still pretending to be my friend," I said, my voice trembling, ignoring Joshua's attempts to calm me down using his signature 'Debs'.

"What are you talking about?" Lucy stood up, staring at me with a mix of fear and confusion.

"I saw you at the mall with him. Don't tell me he has a Tinder twin."

"It's not what you think. He called me. He said you were going through a tough time. He wanted us to repeat what we did together but I told him I was in a committed relationship."

I shifted the Wesson toward Joshua, my hands still shaking. I tried to steady the trembling by holding the gun with both hands, but it didn't help.

"She came onto me," Joshua said, putting Paula Fox down. "She said I was the best she ever had," he added.

The barrel of the Wesson moved back to Lucy, who was now crying.

"We can go back to how things were, Debs. You know how we do it," Joshua said, standing up as Lucy's sobs grew louder. I pulled the trigger and missed by a mile. *I should have practiced in front of people instead of trees*, I thought again, as blood began to pool in our living room.

Lucy was hiccupping loudly, with tributaries of snot going down her face. Meanwhile, I had grown bolder; every inch of me was alert. I grabbed her by the arm. "Listen to me, Lucy," I said sternly. "When the police ask what happened here, you're going to say you visited, we started quarreling, he slapped me, and you left."

"O…okay," she stammered, picking her bag and leaving.

At this point, it would be remiss of me not to mention the craftsmanship of the .38 revolver. Say what you will about Smith & Wesson, but they did a perfect job with the gun. The bullet went clean through Joshua's right ventricle, and he was probably dead before I finished squeezing the trigger. That meant hospitals were out of the question and I was looking at a murder charge. I loved Joshua, but there was no way I was serving time for his death, so I needed to get creative yet again.

After calling the police, I plugged in the iron and started burning my thighs and parts of my arm. But I knew that wouldn't be enough. It took a lot of guts, but I finally managed to convince myself to run full tilt into the wall with a smile on my face. When I looked down, there were four of my incisors on the floor, and a black eye on my left side. I was going to blame everything on Joshua. The bad man who made me do bad things.

You might be thinking by now that I'm a terrible woman, that I deserved everything that happened to me. And I wouldn't blame you. But remember, just like you, I wanted ordinary things, and I was making the best of a bad situation. Joshua was already dead and I had my whole life ahead of me. Besides, he wouldn't be the one walking around with four missing teeth, now would he?

The police found me crying next to the body, with my mouth and nose full of red. They introduced themselves, but my mind was too frazzled to catch their names. For a second, I could not even make out their faces, all I saw were shapes of blue. "I… I didn't mean to do it. It… it was self-defense," I stammered as my mind and vision returned to me. I had ridden my dress up my thighs, exposing my scars for the world to see. *"Pole kwa msiba wako, usijali, kila kitu itakuwa sawa,"* one of the two police officers said, his thick mustache twitching as he spoke.

"Huyu kijana alikuwa jangili. Hata bunduki yake haina serial number," the other police officer added, picking up the .38 with a gloved hand.

"Let me call an ambulance for you," Mr. mustache continued. Thank heavens for the damsel-in-distress act.

I put on a heavy purple coat over my sundress and slipped into black sneakers, and we sped off to Kenyatta National Hospital. There, I was checked, cleaned, and bandaged.

I spent the night at the hospital and the following morning, the police took me into custody at Loresho Police Station. I was placed in a small cell for about 24 hours with three other inmates, who, like me, looked as if they were there 'by mistake,' while I awaited arraignment in court.

This is how it ends, I thought. But that was before Joshua's lawyers visited me. It turned out he had named me in his will, leaving me the house, and a share of his patented thermostat. Every time a unit was sold, I would be cashing checks too. Good old Joshua. *I'm happy I never left.* We then discussed my defense extensively and I put Lucy down as my alibi. I almost grinned, but then I remembered my four missing teeth and decided happiness didn't quite fit into the damsel-in-distress puzzle.

I called Lucy. She was hesitant about testifying, but she quickly changed her mind after I made her an offer she couldn't refuse.

I was arraigned in court on a Tuesday morning in August. The judge, in her white wig and cat-eye glasses, read out my charges:

"How do you plead?" she asked.

"Not guilty," one of my lawyers responded.

I was released on a bail of 750,000 Kenya shillings—a check I signed without hesitation. *What was the price of freedom?* I wondered. I could have signed a check that was 10 times the quoted sum in a heartbeat if that is what it took. Freedom was priceless, I decided.

I spent my days running errands, missing Joshua, and going for lunch dates with Lucy. I would try to do anything and everything to get the thought of prison out of my mind. After the investigating officers filed their report, my lawyers approached me and told me I needed to check into Mathari Mental Hospital.

I'm going crazy and my lawyers know it too, I thought.

I stayed at Mathari for about a week, undergoing dozens of tests. My lawyers filed my defense, and soon we were back in court for the hearing.

The hearing took place on a Monday morning in October. It was a blur, drowned out by the constant ringing in my ears. I remember it in bits and pieces; the prosecuting lawyers representing the government droning on about how I had a motive because I came from a humble background, while Joshua was well-off. According to them, I had everything to gain with him out of the picture.

The judge listened intently, jotting down notes, while one of my lawyers argued that Joshua had been a violent man. Lucy and the police officers who came to my house testified. Before I knew it, I was on the stand, slurring my words because I wasn't used to speaking with four missing teeth. Did I admit my guilt? Did I say Joshua used to beat me often and that what I did was out of self-defense, temporary insanity or both? I don't remember—at least not with clarity. But I do remember the judge announcing she would give her judgment in three months.

I returned to my routine: running errands, missing Joshua, and going on lunch dates with Lucy. Some days, I wanted to check myself back to Mathari because I felt as if I was losing my mind waiting for judgment day.

When the day finally arrived, I stood once more before the judge with the white wig and cat-eye glasses. I was surprised to see my stepbrother in the crowd. I waved at him after a guard removed the handcuffs from my wrists. I certainly remember the verdict with clarity. "Not guilty," the judge boomed, instructing that the bail I had paid be refunded.

Sheesh! I could put a man to the ground every day if this is the slap on the wrist you get, I thought, embracing my lawyers, Lucy and my stepbrother.

In the days that followed, I contacted my gun seller and got myself another Wesson. What? A girl needs protection from the Joshuas of this world. I also got work done on my teeth. You will be surprised at the things money fixes. I would know, with my Colgate ad smile.

Last Sunday

I SOLD THE Loresho bungalow, sent my step-brother some money, and moved to a private villa along the shoreline of Kilifi to start afresh. Joshua's bungalow pales in comparison. My new home is set on a hill overlooking the Indian ocean. It is modernly styled with large glass windows and doors that let in the sun. When you open the doors, the breathtaking flora and fauna, of the breeze from trees, and the songs from birds hug you like a loving mother.

I have been here for almost a year. The January sun is high in the sky, and I keep it from entering the house with black heavy curtains. I am such a contrast to this place. I haven't had a shower or changed my clothes in months. Whenever I have an appetite—which is rare—I order fast food and insist that the rider leave it outside.

It's Sunday. I move slowly and catch my reflection in one of the glass doors. My hair is unkempt, and my clothes are faded, dirty and loose on my body, which is mostly bones. I look like the fabled witches in Ladybird books. I've tried to forget him. Tried to move on and date other men, but like a bad nightmare, he visits me every night.

Lucy called earlier. She keeps insisting on visiting, and we've planned for her to come next month. She asked why my voice was hoarse, and I told her I have a slight cold but it will pass. She got married but is afraid her husband might be using Tinder again. I told her to leave him, but she said leaving was not an option. I suppose she, too, understands that sometimes the stakes are too high to leave.

I walk slowly to my bedroom and remove the Smith & Wesson .38 revolver from my drawer, spinning it on my bedside table. It holds five bullets, but it only has two. Since Friday, I have been adding a bullet, rotating the cylinder, placing it against my temple, and pulling the trigger. Since Friday, all I have been met with is a click.

I add another bullet, rotate the cylinder, and place it on my temple, hopefully for one last time. I can already hear the loud bang and the singing birds fluttering away from the trees. I can envision Lucy's hysteria when she visits and finds my body. I wait for a heartbeat longer before pulling the trigger and wonder—*will today be the day I finally join Joshua for eternity?*

Proverbs 31 Woman

Manicure

I meet her on Thursday at a barbershop in Nairobi's CBD. She's the masseuse washing my head and giving me a massage.

"Kwani ulipotelea wapi?" she asks while I position my head on the washing bowl. I raise my head and look at her. It's not the first time I've seen her. I've noticed her before. She's my type— beautiful, with a tiny waist and wide hips. I often cross my fingers, hoping she'll be the one attending to me, but there's always another masseuse.

"Niko tu, wewe ndio umepotea. Kwani ulienda ushago Christmas?" I ask.

"Nilikuwa tu Nairobi," she replies.

I look at her oval face with big brown eyes. Most girls have sad brown eyes, but hers are kind.

"*Tunafaa tukule* lunch," I say.

"Lunch *nitakulia tu hapa,*" she responds.

Her tone of voice makes her sound like a *mama mboga* in her kiosk, guarding her territory. I remain silent and she starts washing my head. She soaps it, rinses it, and directs me to the massage chair. She oils my scalp, digging her fingers in, and I can feel the stress of the weakening economy leaving my body. She wants to work on my back, but my clothes are in the way.

"*Nitoe* sweater?" I ask.

"*Eh, toa,*" she replies.

I take off my blue sweater and remain with my black t-shirt. She hangs my sweater, grabs a towel, and wraps it around the neck of my t-shirt. Then, she sinks her hands through my clothes and begins applying oil on my shoulders, chest, and back. Her fingers and knuckles dig into my skin. If the stress of the weakening economy had left me before, now it's the stress of bad governance that's melting away.

She tells me to lean forward and kneads my back over my t-shirt, then takes my hands and stretches them so they brush against her small breasts.

"*Usinivunje mikono,*" I tease.

She giggles. "*Siwezi.*"

After she's done, she gets a warm, damp towel and cleans the oil from my head, face, back and chest, then lotions my head and face.

"*Unataka* manicure?" she asks. I think about it for a moment. My nails grow at an alarming rate, and I have to cut them weekly. A manicure won't do any harm.

"*Nani anafanya hiyo* manicure?" I ask.

"*Mimi,*" she says, with the confidence of knowing she's my favorite.

"*Sawa,*" I say expansively.

She takes me to a small manicure room. I sit behind a table and watch her gather her tools. "*Sikuwa nakuona* time *ya* Corona. *Ulikuwa umepotelea wapi?*" I ask as she arranges her tools on the table.

"*Mimi nilikuwa nakuona ukikuja kuulizia* Tom." (Tom was my barber, but he left). But that's neither here nor there. What matters now is that she's been noticing me. All her tools are on the table, she sits across from me. I raise my gaze, and her big brown eyes swallow me up. For the first time, I realize how intimate this is.

She picks my right hand and starts clipping my nails.

"*Nafaa kukubeba ukuwe unakata makucha zangu,*" I say, drowning in her eyes. She smiles—she has this white, endearing smile.

"*Utanibeba tu juu ya makucha?*"

"*Makucha… na kubabysit* TV *na nyumba.*"

She laughs. Her right leg is now pressed against my left leg, and I can feel the voltage between us. She finishes clipping the nails on my right hand and starts filling them. I take a proper look at her. She's in a loose-fitting black dress, her hair pulled back in a ponytail, revealing ears adorned with tiny emerald earrings. Her complexion is like coffee with milk. Her nose is almost a button nose, and her lips are neither bee-stung nor thin. I can't place her ethnicity accurately—she could be Kamba, Luhya or Mijikenda.

"*Unapenda kukula nini?*" I ask?

"*Kuku.*"

"*Wasichana wote* Nairobi *wanapenda kukula kuku,*" I tease.

She laughs again and places my right hand into a bowl of warm water mixed with Dettol, then picks up my left hand. We're having mundane conversation, but there's electricity coursing between our words, and only we can feel it.

"*Haupendi* pizza?" I ask.

"Pizza *hunipea* gas. *Napenda kuku na* milkshake *za* Java," she says.

"*Ni siku gani wewe hutoka* job *mapema?*"

"*Ngai, nilikuwa nadhani unajoke,*" she says.

"*Hakuna* jokes, *sisi ni watu wazima hapa.*"

She looks at me as if sizing me up. I hold her gaze.

"Sunday," she replies.

"*Hauendangi* church Sunday?"

"*Mimi huenda asubuhi.*"

"Church *gani?*"

"Catholic."

"*Wewe huenda* confession? *Hizo dhambi zote za kushika-shika wanaume, Mungu hawezi kusamehe,*" I say teasingly, though I quickly realize how it could come across as an insult.

She flashes her teeth at me, and pushes me to the deep end of her big brown eyes.

"*Hii* Sunday *siko, but hiyo ingine nitakuwa,*" I say.

"*Unajua kupika kweli?*" she teases now, though without realizing it, she's hinting that she's okay with coming to my place without a formal date.

"*Kupika ni kazi rahisi na kuna* Glovo," I respond.

"*Unaweza chinja kuku kweli?*"

"*Wewe huwezi chinja kuku?*" I throw the ball back in her court.

"*Mimi naogopa.* So *unaweza kumuua mtu?*" she asks.

I laugh. "*Mtu ana hisia. Mtu huongea. Kuua mtu si kitu rahisi,*" I say.

She dips my left hand into the bowl, towels my right hand, and begins removing the cuticles. Her leg is still pressed against mine. I lose myself in her face and think, *I will enjoy having you.*

"*Uko na mikono* soft," she says.

I hold her hand and rub her fingers against mine. Her nails are painted black.

"*Hizi mikono hufight?*" I ask.

She shakes her head.

"*Hazijawai chapa msichana juu ya mwanaume?*"

"*Heri nipike chai nikunywe,*" she replies.

I laugh. "*Unajua mikono zinaweza kuambia* age *ya mtu?*" I say.

She looks at me curiously.

"*Unaweza* guess *niko na miaka ngapi?*" I ask.

"*Wewe?* You look like you're still building your empire," she says. I smile, liking the way she says that because it acknowledges the existence of an empire (which I may be oblivious to), and it suggests there's room for her to contribute to it. "*Naweza sema* 30, 31."

"31 in June," I say, delighted by her intuition. I take her hand again, ready to guess her age.

"*Uko* ready?" I ask.

"*Aki, usiniambie. Ukisema* age *siyo hiyo, nitakasirika,*" she warns.

"26," I say without preamble, and she glows.

"You're right."

She goes quiet for a moment, working on my hand, then speaks again.

"*Unajua mtu akikuona anaweza kufikiria uko* 26, but *ukiongea, mtu anajua wewe ni mzee.*"

I should stay silent more often and shave five years from my age, easy. I think.

"*Wewe ni* firstborn?" she asks.

"*Mimi ni* third born. Last born *ni* agemate *yako.*"

"*Msichana?*"

"*Eh, wazazi wangu ni wazee,*" I say finally.

She's now toweling my left hand and removing the cuticles.

"*Naitwa* Brian," I say.

"I'm Abby," she says.

"*Umewahi ingia kwa duka ukapata kiatu* size *yako, na hiyo kiatu inakaa poa?*" I'm turning the charm all the way up. "*Ukipata kiatu kama hiyo, si unatoa pesa bila kuambiwa?*"

"*Eh*. But *kwanza niambie*. Do you have a wife and kids?" she asks.

I let her big brown eyes swallow me again.

"That's where you come in," I say.

One of her colleagues enters the room and sits on the adjacent sofa while Abby is polishing my nails with a soft sponge, and we quiet down. But even in silence, there's electricity in the room. Even someone without their senses could feel the voltage between us.

I take my phone from my pocket, open the dial-pad, and push it towards Abby, making sure her colleague can't see. She keys in her number and taps the green button so she has mine too. I pick up my phone from the table and slide it back into my pocket. The colleague, seated on the sofa, gets up and leaves, perhaps realizing that three is a crowd.

"*Sitakuwa hii* weekend, but I will be around the next one," I remind her.

"*Nitakuja nione ukipika,*" she says.

"*Ukikam, unajua kutawaka moto.*"

It's that blinding smile again, and those big brown eyes.

My phone starts ringing. I have a meeting scheduled for noon. Talking to this girl, time seems to be flying.

"I gotta get going, Abby. *Tutaongea* next week," I say.

"*Ungeniambia uko na* meeting *ningeharakisha; ni vile ulianza kunipigisha* story," she says, bringing out a salt-like substance and massaging my hand with quick, fluid movements.

I get up.

"Brian, *sijamaliza*. I think I have missed something," she says, inspecting my nails and toweling my hands."

"*Utamaliza tukipatana*," I say with a cheeky smile as she lotions my hands. I pick up my sweater and look around in case I've left something. "*Kama nimesahau kitu, utaniambia*," I say, walking to the reception desk. I pay and glance around the barbershop. They all look oblivious. A nuclear bomb just exploded right under their noses, and they didn't even notice.

I step out of the barbershop and save her number into my contacts. I head down the stairs with a skip in my step. You know, we're so used to meeting lovers on the internet that meeting them the old-fashioned way feels refreshing. I get out of the building and take a breath of fresh air. I also smell something else. I sometimes get these moments when I can faintly feel the future, and this time, I catch a whiff of her love box during our future lovemaking.

Rehearsals

I ARRIVE AT my two-bedroom house in Kasarani, and the first thing I do is check Abby's profile on social media. A woman's profile is often revealing. It offers you a glimpse into her character. This is where I can determine if she is self-absorbed and full of hubris or well-adjusted.

Her bio says she loves cooking and she's a Proverbs 31 woman. I open the verse in the Bible, coughing from the dust because I haven't touched it in a while. *She is clothed with strength and dignity; she can laugh at the days to come. She speaks with wisdom, and faithful instruction is on her tongue. She watches over the affairs of her household and does not eat the bread of idleness.*

I like the sound of that. Bread of idleness? Yuck. I save one of Abby's pictures and stare at it. Those big brown eyes, chiseled oval face, that figure—we have chemistry. *It's high time I got a wife and built a family,* I think, *and this one will do nicely.*

I let my mind wander. I try out my second name with her first name to see how they fit together. I decide that it suits her. I imagine the vacations, playful moments, and our future kids. But while I'm thinking about this, my thoughts take a detour, and I start imagining her touching all those men in her job as a masseuse. I don't like the taste in my mouth. Once she properly settles into my last name, she'll have to leave that job. I decide.

Throughout the week, I keep looking at the photo I downloaded of Abby and stalking her social media. She doesn't post much, if at all, which strikes me as very Proverbs-31-woman-like. There's another woman who calls me often. I put their photos side by side and decide the other one doesn't stand a chance.

I don't text Abby throughout the week, even though I'm dying to. I don't want to dilute the chemistry we built. I want the idea of me—of us—to smolder in her mind, so that when I text her next week, the smolder will ignite into an inferno.

Next week arrives, and I text her on a Wednesday evening.

"*Hawayu.*"

I check my phone furiously. 30 minutes pass, then 45, then an hour. Nothing. Well, goodbye Proverbs 31 woman.

"Hi Brian…" The text pops up after two hours, and I breathe a sigh of relief.

"For a minute, *nilidhani umemeza ulimi,*" I reply, hoping she'll laugh and I can text back. "…*Nikashangaa utakulaje kuku bila ulimi.*" And she can laugh some more but she goes quiet again. *Who tells people wamemeza ulimi?* Idiot.

"*Ni vile niko* home. I rarely touch my phone," Abby's reply comes an hour later. "When did you say you get out of work the earliest?" I decide to go for goal.

"Sundays, 3:00 p.m…"

"But this Saturday I won't be working…"

"Let's have our chicken Sato then." I jump at the opportunity.

"Haha, okay."

"*Utaniambia* time."

"*Sawa.*"

After she accepts, I'm ecstatic. I feel like the cock of the walk. At that moment, I could have taken on the world, and it wouldn't have stood a chance. I don't confirm the date or location just yet. I decide to wait till Friday evening and kill two birds with one stone—give her the details and confirm we're still on at the same time.

Thursday comes, and all I can do is stare at Abby's photo and giggle to myself. There are those big brown eyes, chiseled oval face, that figure—and we have chemistry. *It's high time I got a wife and built a family, and this one will do nicely,* I replay the thought.

I listen to Mbosso's Sonona: *Ewe binti maringo, sijui wanisikia. Pendo lako nicheze bingo. Huenda nikajishindia. Mwenzako bado niko single. Pendo limenichachia…* Love songs are starting to make sense.

Friday morning comes. I wake up, piss, flush, wash my hands, and have breakfast. I put on music and start cleaning in my gray boxers and baggy Safaricom t-shirt. I wash dishes, do laundry, and put blankets on the line to get some sun. I clean my bedroom, then wash the other bedroom that doubles as my office. I wash the kitchen… There's a lot of washing happening.

I wash the bathroom, getting down on my knees to scrub the toilet. Then I move on to the living room. There's a spot on the ceiling where dust collects; I grab a broom, sweep it down, and watch as it all falls to the floor. It takes me about an hour to clean everything up, after I'm done, the house is spotless. I know from experience to prepare for success. You don't want a girl looking at your dusty walls and wondering what else might be dusty about you.

The clock reads 5:00 p.m. I change into my black running tracksuit, get my headphones, mask, and hit the tarmac. Nyashinski is in my ear: *Africa tunaikamia tu mos mos bana. I'm Kenyan so you know I'm a marathon runner...*

I get back at around 6:00 p.m., take a shower, change into light gray pajamas, and have rice and beef stew for supper as I switch the TV between YouTube and Netflix. By the time I put down my clean plate, the stars are already in the sky. I pick my phone and text Abby, fingers crossed. *What if she made other plans? Well, I'll have resilience and a clean house.'*

"Hey, let's meet at 12:00 p.m., *kesho* at Garden City Mall. Doing some shopping, then we can grab some chicken and head to my place," I text. A woman wants to feel that you'll be okay whether she comes or not. If she even senses that your life depends on her coming, she won't come.

"Hi…latest 12:30, I'm not good with keeping time."

Abby's text comes after 20 minutes. I get quite irate with people who can't keep time, but I give her that one. It seems more like an attempt at humor than anything else. Besides, you can't really be late if you let someone know beforehand.

"You can do 12:31. Now you've got all the time in the world," I reply.

She laughs.

"Okay… See you tomorrow."

"I hope you're doing well, Brian."

"We'll talk tomorrow. Goodnight."

"See you tomorrow. Goodnight."

Sometimes, my cock panics when it sees rubber, so I had planned to try on a condom—call it rehearsals. Abby is the kind of girl I'd be happy just sitting and talking with because we actually have chemistry. But, like I mentioned before, it's important to prepare for success.

There is a pack of Durex with a single condom left in my wardrobe. I pick it up and lie on my bed, staring at the ceiling. Honestly, I don't feel like doing this; all that cleaning and running has left me exhausted. But I need to get through it. I open my phone and tap on Abby's photo. A few indecent thoughts cross my mind, and soon enough, my cock starts stiffening. I slide the condom on. I haven't touched myself in a while, and the sensation feels pretty good. I consider stroking myself and finishing in the condom, but I decide to save it for the main event.

Anxious

I WAKE UP at around 8:00 a.m., and head to the bathroom. I piss, wash my hands, and have breakfast—two eggs, three slices of bread, and a cup of tea. I put on some music and start cleaning the spots I missed yesterday. *Cheerleader* by Omi fills the house: *Oh, I think that I found myself a cheerleader, she is always right there when I need her...* I grab a damp cloth and wipe down the sockets and switches. Squatting, I clean the dust along the line where the tiles meet the wall.

I try wiping the handwashing sink next to the toilet with the damp cloth, but the stains won't budge. *Leave something for her to clean,* I tell myself, but on second thought, I fill a bucket halfway with water, pour in some Persil, and grab a brush. By the time I'm done, the sink is sparkling white.

It's now 10:00 a.m., and Tiwa Savage is in my ear: *Mister lover lover, you know say I no get wahala. Anyhow you like, I go do my dear as long as you no cause palava...* I take a duster and go over the house again. Then, I grab the white sneakers I plan to wear and start cleaning them. That's when anxiety hits me, hard, like a mallet.

All of a sudden, I'm nervous. Will I still be attracted to her? You know how people can look and seem one way in one setting and be completely different in another. I take the laces out of my shoes and wash them. After drying them with a towel, I put them out in the sun.

I hop in the shower, turn on the faucet, soap up, rinse, and towel off. I apply Nivea Cocoa Glow on my skin, spray Nivea Fresh Active Deo on my armpits, and put on a white vest. Then, I spray on some Nivea Men Deep Black Charcoal and slip into an orange t-shirt and blue denim jeans over my black boxers. I pull on my blue socks, and sink into my shoes. The look is finished off with my watch and spectacles. I check myself in the mirror—I look good, some might even say edible.

It's now 11:30 a.m., and Diamond's *Sikomi* is playing in my ears, but it's doing nothing to help my anxiety. My palms are sweaty as I dial for an Uber. After I'm done giving the Uber driver directions, I pick up an empty bottle of Keringet water and place it by the door. I'm also planning to do some shopping at Carrefour—or did my anxiety make you forget?

I toggle the music to bedroom songs to set the mood. Bobby Valentino comes on: *Slow down, never seen anything so lovely. Now turn around and bless me with your beauty…* The playlist is an hour and 46 minutes long—more than enough time for me to pick up Abby, do my shopping, and get back.

The Uber arrives after 15 minutes. I grab the empty Keringet water bottle and head out.

It's 11:45 a.m., when I reach Garden City Mall. The anxiety is still there, but it's ebbing. I stop by Carrefour and punch in the Keringet water bottle at the Customer Service desk. I shove the receipt into my back pocket and head over to the liquor section to buy condoms.

You never want a woman to see you buying condoms in her honor. At least not when you're just starting to interact. She might be upset, and the sex might not happen. Women want to believe that sex just happened—spontaneous, unplanned, and neither of you had it in mind.

I pick up the condoms, tuck them into my pocket, and head to an M-Pesa booth. It's noon, and my phone rings. It's Abby.

"I'm already here," she says.

"Meet me at the entrance to Carrefour," I reply, ending the call. I thought we agreed she'd be here at 12:31 p.m.—I still have things to take care of. I need to get some cash and head to the washrooms to unwrap this box of condoms. They usually wrap them like they're hiding nuclear codes, and the last thing I want is to fumble with it in front of her. I feel slightly irritated that she didn't stick to her time, but then again, it's good that she's early. It means she's eager to spend more time with me.

I withdraw 1,000 Kenya shillings and head to the washrooms. It takes me about two minutes to wrestle the Durex box open. Finally, I get the three condom packets, slip them into my pocket, toss the box in the waste bin, wash my hands, and go looking for my flame.

"*Niko* Carrefour. Where are you?" I ask her on the phone.

"*Nilienda kununua maji.* I'm at the counter," she says.

I spot Abby at the quick check-out counter, and the view is worth it. Her hair is in freshly done braids, tied into a ponytail with a black hairband. She's wearing hula-hoop earrings that dangle from her earlobes. Her short, slim-fitting purple dress ends just above her knees, revealing her brown thighs, and her feet are tucked into small black ankle boots.

When I saw her sitting at the manicure table before, she looked much taller than me, and I'd imagined she was bigger. Now, standing here, I realize she's shorter, and I'm towering over her. I give her a hug.

"I was thirsty, *nikaona ninunue maji,*" Abby says, holding her Mt. Kenya bottle of water and giving me a glance with those big brown eyes and her slightly made-up face, which accentuates her beauty.

"*Ninanunua maji pia*," I say, getting a trolley. The anxiety has vanished, and we stroll through the aisles together. She's still holding her Mt. Kenya water bottle, but as soon as I place the Keringet bottle in the trolley, she hurries to return hers to the shelf.

"Oh, *wacha nirudishe hii,*" she says.

I pick up a packet of 12 Tena toilet rolls and a pack of six Frusion yogurt.

"That's it, *nimemaliza*," I say.

"*Ungefanya hii* shopping *baadaye*," she says as we approach the counter and check out.

As we step outside, I reach into my pocket and hand Abby a thousand bob. "*Enda ununue* Streetwise 2 *mbili* KFC." I'm killing two birds with one stone—I can order the Uber while also seeing how she handles my money. I know a Streetwise 2 is 350 Kenya shillings. She should have at least 300 Kenya shillings in balance. Even though I've already decided she can keep the change, I'm curious to see if she'll mention it.

I dial the Uber; it's waiting in the parking lot. I load the shopping into the boot, sit up front with the driver, and wait for Abby. She's taking her time, so I strike up a conversation to keep him distracted from the wait.

We start talking about the afterlife. The Uber driver claims that when people die, they go to other planets. I tell him I doubt it, because planets are physical places. Our technology isn't advanced enough to reach them yet, but maybe someday it will be.

"How long will you be?" I call Abby.

"*Wamesema* 15 minutes."

Another car wants to leave and we are on the way, we move ahead and park a bit further down.

"*Wewe unataka kusema watu wanaendanga wapi wakikufa?*" the driver asks.

"Souls *ziko na sisi huku tu.* That's why *unaskianga mtu akisema alikuwa amelala akaona* someone who died a long time ago," I respond.

I dial Abby again. "How long now?"

"I am on my way," she replies.

Five minutes later, she calls. "*Niko hapa kwa* ATMs."

I get out, fetch her, and open the back door for her.

"For a minute *nilidhani* KFC *inakuona inasonga,*" I joke.

The Uber driver laughs. I was fishing for that laugh, you'd think he is the one I'm taking home.

He starts the car, and we're off. He's chatty throughout the journey, and I'm beginning to regret starting the conversation.

"*Ati mnaongea kuhusu nini?*" Abby asks from the back seat.

"*Tunaongea kuhusu kifo. Watu huenda wapi wakikufa?*" I tell her.

She goes silent.

"*Nasema* souls *ziko huku tu nasisi, hakuna pahali zimeenda,*" I explain.

"*Eh,*" she chirps softly from the back.

"*Hapana, watu wanaenda* planets *zingine*," the driver insists.

We reach the gate, and the conversation with the driver finally comes to an end. Thank you, God. I pay him via M-Pesa, grab the shopping from the boot, and lead the way. Just as I reach the stairs, I notice Abby is lagging behind. I stop and call out, "*Kuja ubebe hizi.*" I hand her the bag with the tissue paper and Frusion yogurt, while I carry the Keringet.

As she takes the bag, I notice a couple of house-helps in the compound staring at us. We climb the stairs, and I turn the key to house number 10 on the first floor. The moment the door opens, Chris Brown's voice fills the space: *Yo, tell me fellas have you seen her? It was about five minutes ago. When I seen the hottest chick that a youngin' ever seen before… I gotta give her game proper. Spit it, so she get it, there she is, I gotta stop her…*

Questions

I REMOVE MY shoes and take the Keringet water to the kitchen. When I return, I find Abby sitting on the arm of my two-seater sofa, removing her shoes.

"Floor *yako ni baridi*," she exclaims.

"*Unataka* socks?"

"*Hapana.* I'll just wear the ones I have."

She has tiny black socks meant for her ankle boot heels. I head to the bedroom and remove my blue socks, which go all the way to my knees. I don't need that kind of discomfort in this January heat. I switch to orange ankle socks, take the condoms from my pocket and stash them in the bottom drawer of my wardrobe. Then, I return to the living room, where Abby is now seated on the sofa, and the chicken still wrapped in the KFC bag on the coffee table.

"Do you want to serve the chicken?" I ask.

She gets up and heads to the kitchen. I hear the sound of her washing her hands. Then, she's back on the sofa with the bag.

"*Nimeamua hatutatumia* plates. *Tusichafue vyombo za* bachelor," she says, staring at me with those big brown eyes. She blinks. When her eyelids close and then open, it feels like pulling back the curtains on a large window with a scenic view. I allow myself to get lost in the view before tearing open the brown bag to serve as a mat on the sofa.

Aubrey is in our ears with Fire & Desire: *You just like my sidekick, I just wanna wife, fulfill all your desires. Keep you in the front, never in the back, and never on the side…*

"Is the music too loud? *Nipunguze* volume?" I ask while opening my box of KFC chicken.

"*Iko sawa,*" Abby says as I start eating. I notice she's not eating, she's just staring at me.

"Do you have a tattoo?" she asks.

"No," I reply.

"*Unakaa* the type that would have one," she says, shifting her gaze to the painting on the wall. It's a large painting of two glasses of wine—. one with white wine, the other with red. The wine spills from both glasses and meets in the middle to form a heart. I find it quite poetic.

"I love your painting," she says.

"*Ebu* guess *nilibuy* how much?" My ego can't resist asking.

"20,000?"

I shake my head.

"30,000?"

I shake my head.

"45,000?"

"6,000," I finally say, having had enough of her guesses and her jaw drops.

"I know, I feel as if I stole it," I add, deciding that from now on, I'll tell people it's worth 50,000 Kenya shillings.

Her eyes land on my brown wooden coffee table, where *An Anonymous Girl* sits. She picks up the book.

"So, *wewe husoma?*"

"Sometimes."

"*Nimeona wewe* ni Ben Carson," she says, probably having seen the stack of books on my desk when she passed by my office bedroom. I laugh. "*Na wewe*, do you read?"

"Not often. I think *nilisoma kitabu moja* last year, *na hata sikumaliza.*"

I put a drumstick in my mouth and pull out a clean bone.

"It's easier *kusoma ukiwa peke yako*, I guess."

I throw the bone into my box.

"So, *wewe hufanya kazi gani?*" she asks while biting a French fry.

"I'm a creative," I say.

"Creative *wa nini?*"

"I write." I pause. "I write for brands." It's a half-truth. I also write novels, short stories, and poetry.

"Brands *gani?*"

I tell her and start eating the second piece of chicken. Her questions are relentless.

"*Uko na* hobbies *gani?*"

"*Kusoma si ni* hobby," I reply, finishing my chicken.

"*Umeshiba hiyo kuku kweli?*"

"*Eh.*"

"*Venye umebeba hiyo maji mzito na ukangojea kwa hiyo jua?*"

"*Nilikuwa ndani ya gari, na hiyo maji hata si mzito.*"

"*Eh, kama ni mimi ningeambia mtu anisaidie. Unataka nikuletee maji ya kunywa?*"

"*Eh.*"

I love how she gets up without hesitating and brings me a glass of water from the dispenser. It's a small gesture, but it makes me feel appreciated and respected. I take the glass and down it in one quick swig.

"Supper *utapika saa ngapi?*" she asks.

"*Jioni*, around 8:00 p.m.," I respond.

"*Eh, nitakuwa nimeshaenda* but *nataka kuona ukipika.*"

"*Kupika haina* formula. *Tunanunua nyama nusu hapa. Naiboil* for an hour. *Nakaranga. Natengeneza ugali. Hiyo* story *tunamaliza.*"

The look on her face tells me she doesn't believe me.

"*Ama unataka tununue kuku tuchinje?*" I ask.

"*Unaweza chinja kuku?*"

"*Wewe huwezi chinja kuku?*"

"*Mimi naogopa*" she pauses. "So *unaweza kuua mtu?*"

"*Kuchinja kuku na kuua mtu sio* the same.*"

"*Heh. Mimi siwezi.*"

"*Unataka kunywa* yogurt?" I ask, switching gears. She nods. "*Enda ulete hizo* Frusion yogurt *nimebuy.*"

We both make to get up but before we do, my lips part again. "*Uko na watoto wangapi?*" I ask, curiosity getting the better of me. I can see her figure, and I know other men are not blind to it.

"*Mmoja tu,*" she says, and my heart sinks.

"A boy or a girl?"

"A boy."

My heart sinks further. I prefer girls. Sometimes I'm a bit of a dick to my dad, and he's my real dad. I can only imagine how it would be if he were a step-dad—I probably wouldn't give him the time of day.

"*Na wewe? Uko na watoto?*"

"*Sina.*"

"Perfect," Abby says as she gets up. I follow suit and head to the sink in the corridor leading to the kitchen. I wash my hands a bit longer waiting for her to come from the kitchen. It's time I smacked that big ass of hers and got this party started. I dry my hands and wait. She walks past me, and I pretend I'm still finishing up. I follow her and give her a smack. It jiggles in my hand.

"Brian, *nani amekuambia unispank kama hujaomba ruhusa?*" Abby says, sitting down and handing me a cup of Frusion yogurt and a spoon. I smile. It would be a sad day if an ass like that walked around this house unsmacked.

"*Nani hufua nguo zako?*" she asks.

"*Songa karibu nikuambie,*" I say, opening my Peach & Apricot yogurt. The plan is to dip a finger inside, smear it on her lips, and kiss her. It's as if she senses it, because she immediately gets up and moves to sit on the armchair of the sofa.

"*Mm mm, nijibu kwanza.*"

"Sometimes *mimi hufua*, other times, *mimi huita mama fua.*"

"*Wewe hukunywa pombe?*"

"*Sijakunywa pombe* in a while."

"*Ama wewe hukunywa wasichana?*"

Women will finish you long before you finish them. No one man can have them all—not even King Solomon could. I stay silent for a moment.

"It's either *unakunywa wasichana, ama* you're focused on your career," she continues. "*Ama nakuuliza maswali mingi sana?*"

I spoon my Peach & Apricot. "*Umeniuliza maswali ya kutosha. Sasa ni* time *yangu kukujua.* But I will do it differently." Sade's *Sweetest Taboo* is playing in the background: *If I tell you how I feel, will you keep bringing out the best in me… You give me, the sweetest taboo…*

"Hey Google, pause music," I say, without preamble. Google doesn't ask me why; the living room just goes quiet.

"*Funga macho.*" Abby closes her eyes without hesitation.

"I'm going to do a personality test on you, called The Cube, is that okay?" She nods. It's something I learned from Neil Strauss in his book, *The Game.*

"Imagine an empty room," I tell her. "Have you imagined the room?" She nods. "Put a cube in that room. Where in the room have you put it, in the corner or the center?"

"Close to the corner," she says.

"What size is the cube? Is it big or small?"

"It's not too big."

"Is it on the ground or is it floating?"

"It's on the ground."

"What color is the cube?"

"Brown."

"Now, put a ladder in that room."

"I have."

"Where in the room is the ladder?"

"It's far away from the cube."

"What is it made of, rope *ama chuma?*"

"*Chuma.*"

"Now, put a horse in the room."

"I have."

"What is the horse doing?"

"It's just there, doing nothing."

"Does it have a saddle, so you can sit on it and ride?"

"No."

"Open your eyes. Let me tell you what it all means."

She opens her eyes. There is that scenic view again.

"The cube represents your personality. It's close to the corner and not in the center because you don't like a lot of attention. The fact that it's brown instead of transparent or a brighter color shows that you often keep to yourself and don't open up easily. Since it's on the ground, it means you prefer things planned out and don't do well with last-minute changes. Creative people usually imagine their cubes floating."

I pause to let her process the information before continuing.

"The ladder represents your friends. Because it's far from the cube, it means you don't have many close friends or don't see them often. But the relationship is strong since the ladder is made of iron, not something fragile like rope."

She's nodding, her eyes widening slightly.

"The horse symbolizes your potential partner. The fact that it's just standing there means the men in your life, or the ones pursuing you, don't seem to be going anywhere. And since the horse doesn't have a saddle, it indicates that you're not interested in being with these men."

Her jaw slowly drops as I finish explaining, her eyes fixed on me with growing surprise.

"*Wewe ni* mind reader?" Abby asks, moving from the armchair to sit next to me, as if hypnotized. "Because I like to keep to myself. *Na sina marafiki wengi. Sisi huongea* when someone is in need of money, *ama kuna chama.*"

I reach for her arm and gently pull her towards me. She comes without resistance. I dip a finger into my yogurt and smear it lightly around her lips. Leaning in, our lips meet, and there's a spark immediately they lock together. My hand reaches for her purple hairband, pulling it off, and her braids tumble onto her face. I brush them back, and we continue, deeper into the French kiss. My hand slides to her thigh, pushing her purple minidress up slightly. As I move my hand between her thighs, she pushes it away.

We keep kissing, lost in the moment. Abby's hands move to my head, guiding it to her neck, and she trails her lips to my ear, nibbling it softly. The sensation of her warm lips and saliva on my ear sends shivers through me. I kiss her neck, and she responds by pressing my head closer. I bite her skin gently, and she lets out a soft moan, the sound growing louder as I bite a little harder.

My hand slips back between her thighs, brushing against her panties, but after a brief moment, she pushes it away again.

I take off my spectacles and we French some more. My hand finds Abby's inner thighs once more, and I push her panties to the side and brush against flesh and brittle pubic hair. I lift her up and place her on top of me. She removes my orange t-shirt and pushes the hem of my vest behind my neck. Her purple dress is rolled up all the way to her chest, and I'm unhooking her animal print bra. The bra is off and I have one of her nipples in my mouth. She lifts her hands and the dress is off too. We are skin to skin.

I reach for my belt, unbuckle, and whip out my cock. It's stiff. She takes the length of it in her mouth. If I was stiff before, I'm rock hard now.

You get such a good view of a woman when she's taking you in her mouth. I trace her face with a finger and run a hand through her braids. "Go and get the condoms from the bottom drawer of my wardrobe," I tell Abby in a lazy, sexually charged voice." My words fall on deaf ears. She's back on top of me, and I have a nipple in my mouth while my cock rubs against her red panties. I push them aside, and she moves her waist, swallowing me into her wetness.

Honeypots are all different. Sometimes you put your cock in, and it takes a turn. Other times, you don't even know if you're in there. Yet, others grip you and don't let you go until you give her your seed. This one has a grip, even though I have been gripped better, to the point where I was spilling my seed in a minute or less. But those were the days when I was a boy.

She moves up and down the length of me, with my hands assisting her, and my teeth sinking into her neck. I bite her so hard I can see my teeth marks on her skin. She pulls me away from her neck, then pushes me back in again, as if she wants me to bite her, yet at the same time, she doesn't want me to. I find this strange.

She is facing the window, and loud moans are escaping her. I wonder if the house-helps we saw while coming in can hear her. That would be quite the piece of gossip for a while.

My teeth are in her skin, my hands on her ass, and she's swallowing me and spitting me out. The tempo increases. I succumb to her grip and I give her my seed.

"We were not supposed to have sex today, Brian," Abby groans in my ear.

"When were we supposed to have it?" I ask, while removing the hem of my vest from the back of my neck.

"Next year," she says, laughing.

I pick up my spectacles from her side of the sofa as she peels off from me. They are broken; she must have sat on them in the heat of the moment. She now wears a worried look.

"Don't worry. I have another pair."

I go to the bedroom and get them. When I return, I find her seated on the sofa in a daze.

"Ni nini?" I ask.

"Akili yangu imefunguka sasa," she says, looking up at me. "You look so young when you wear spectacles," she adds.

"Unataka kuwatch movie?"

"Let me shower *kwanza*," she says, removing her hula-hoop earrings, and placing them on the coffee table as she heads to the bathroom.

"*Uko na* towel *ingine?*" she asks

The other one is dirty in the bucket.

"*Tumia hiyo iko hapo,*" I say.

After Abby is gone, the magnitude of what I have just done hits me like a train. I realize how much I don't want a kid at this moment. I put my hands on my temples, and wonder how I will broach the P2 subject with her.

"*Uko na* t-shirt *naweza vaa?*" she asks from the bedroom.

"*Kuna* t-shirts *ziko hapo unaweza vaa.*"

She comes to the living room, looking worried.

"Wardrobe *yako iko* empty?"

I don't like clutter, so I don't have a lot of clothes. I give them away as they wear out, so that I just have maybe five good t-shirts and three good trousers.

"*Angalia kwa hiyo* drawer *ya kwanza, kuna* long-sleeved *safi unaweza vaa.*"

Abby comes back to the living room. The t-shirt could be longer but her wide hips won't allow it.

"*Hii ni fupi na hatujafika place ya kuonana tukitembea uchi kwa nyumba.*"

She goes to the bedroom and comes back with a pillow.

"*Naweza tumia hii?*"

I nod.

She crosses her legs and puts the pillow on her lap and starts eating her chicken as I put on *Venom* on Netflix.

"Are you clean?" I ask her.

"*Wewe ndio nafaa kuuliza hiyo swali. Nimeona* condom *imefunguliwa kwa* drawer *yako.*"

How do I start telling her I opened that pack at the mall for convenience?

"But *sijui mbona nimekutrust.* I just feel comfortable with you," she continues while eating her chicken.

Attraction and comfort are the same thing. When you're attracted to someone, regardless of how they might be, you're comfortable with them, and as an effect, you give them your trust out of leniency. I know better, yet here I am, making the same mistake as she is.

"*Nilikuambia uende* condom *ukakataa.*"

"*Nani alikuwa na* time *ya kwenda huko kwote.* Mood *ingekuwa imeisha.*"

She finishes her chicken, and we settle in to watch *Venom.* I'm seated on the couch with my feet on the floor, and she's next to me with her feet crossed on the sofa. The pillow is doing a bad job covering her thick thighs, and my t-shirt is doing an even worse job because I can see her red panties. I trace a finger on her thigh and tag at her panty, aroused.

"*Twende* bed," I groan in a sexually charged voice.

"*Enda peke yako,*" she says.

A few minutes into watching *Venom*, we start remembering that we were having Frusion yogurt before things got heated. We wonder where our cups went when she spots mine spilled over the crevice on my side of the sofa. Hers fell over the sofa and it's in the corner by the window.

We clean up and settle down to watch the movie. I'm sitting on the couch and she's seated next to me when, without preamble, she sinks her hands around my waist and places her head on my chest. It makes me feel good. I love the way she takes refuge in me, as if I am her pillar of strength.

"*Twende* bed?" It's the sexually charged voice again.

She nods, and leads the way. I stay behind to put on some bedroom music. Lil Boosie comes through the speakers with *Calling Me*: *That pussy keeps callin' me... I know I can't love her but that pussy keep callin' me... Get me in trouble...*

Pillow Talk

I GET IN BED, and we start kissing. Abby's lips find my ear, and begin nibbling on it. She pushes the hem of my vest behind my head as my teeth sink into her neck. Lying on my back, she takes the length of me in her mouth. The bed faces the window, the drapes are pulled back. The sun filters in, casting soft light across her face, creating a view that could rival the painting in my living room.

She climbs on top of me, swallowing and spitting me out for about a minute before fatigue sets in, and she gestures for us to switch positions. I take her the way the missionaries do, gazing at her as I give her all of me. Her eyes are squeezed shut, soft moans escaping her lips.

I turn her over, taking her from behind. Another view that rivals my painting. Gripping the bed's headboard, I push deeper into her core. Jeremih is on the speakers with *Birthday Sex*: *You say you want passion, I think you found it. Get ready for action, don't be astounded. We switchin' positions, you feel surrounded...* She's moaning so loudly that I almost want to cover her mouth to muffle the sound. *All that running is finally counting for something.* I think as I slow down the tempo, lying atop her, her eyes remain closed, and she lets out soft, breathy moans.

"Open your eyes," I say.

They remain shut.

"Look at me," I plead.

Nothing.

I give her the length of me for a while before lying on my back beside her. She turns to her side, rests her hand on my waist and lays her head on my chest.

"*Watu wanaonanga kijana amenyamaza, kumbe ni farasi,*" she says.

I look at her and laugh.

"The ladies we passed *tukiingia kwa* gate. You're not worried about them?"

She's referring to the househelps.

"*Mbona?*"

"*Hawatasema* they saw you with a lady?"

"*Hatuongeangi.* So, it doesn't matter." I fall into her eyes. "*Mbona hutaki kuniangalia* when I'm inside you?"

"*Sitaki kushinda nikifikiria tu wewe na* sex." She pauses then continues, "*Unajua, sikuwa nadhani hata unaongeanga.*"

"*Mbona?*"

"*Wewe hukuja, unanyolewa, unaishia.* But *ni poa juu napenda machali wamenyamaza.*"

I'm drowning in her big brown eyes the whole time she's talking.

"When was the last time *ulifanya* manicure?"

"*Kitambo.*"

"*Nani alikufanyia?*"

"*Mama mzee.*"

She gets up and points a finger at me.

"Brian, *usiwahi fanya* manicure *tena.*"

I laugh out loud.

"*Hii ni kitanda ya uchoyo,*" she says without preamble.

My bed is a small three by six. Enough for me.

"*Kila kitu kwa hii nyumba ni ya uchoyo. Hii kitanda,* bathroom *uko na* towel *moja,* sofa *ni* two seater. *Unaletanga* slay queens *kwa hii kitanda kweli?*"

"Slay queens *ni akina nani?*"

"*Madem wa* a good time, not a long time." She gets up and pauses in a way that a slay queen might pause and adjusts her voice to a twang. "Brayo, me I can't sleep in this small bed with you, *nataka* space."

Churchill should come and get this girl. She's a comedian.

"*Wewe unaweza bembeleza dem?*" she asks, settling back onto my chest. "*Uko na ka-ego fulani. Sidhani unaweza bembeleza dem,*" she answers her own question. "Maybe *hii kitanda inafaa kukaa* so we can be closer," she says and we start kissing again.

Her mouth finds my ear, nibbling at it, while my teeth sink into her neck. She lies on her side, and we spoon as Ginuwine plays softly in the background: *Lookin' good, plenty tight. Is there any more room for me in those jeans...* I take her in the missionary position again, and give her the length of me. And then it hits me—the scent I sensed in my fleeting vision. It lingers in every woman, but carries a unique note in each one.

Her moans grow louder as I pick up the tempo, her grip tightening around my cock, overwhelming me. I'm making sounds too—like an injured boar or a dying bull. Just as I'm about to give her my seed again, she grabs my arms. "Don't cum. Don't cum," she barks. I collapse beside her, the intensity fading. *No man can truly master the* WAP, I conclude, as the heat subsides.

"*Utameza* P2?" I ask shamelessly.

"Period *yangu nikuisha inaisha,*" she touches the tip of my cock with her purple nail. "*Hata nashangaa mbona hauna damu,*" she says and removes the hem of my vest from the back of my neck. "*Hii* vest *itakunyonga.*"

She rests her hand on my waist and lays her head on my chest.

"When was the last time *ulikuwa* in a relationship?"

"Situationship."

"What happened?"

"She was dodgy. *Ananiambia* she's around but she's off to Mombasa with another man."

"Awww. I can't believe someone can do something wrong to you. You're so good," she says in that way women do that make men feel spineless. "*Kwani hukuwa unampeleka* vacations?"

I stay quiet.

"If it was me, *natoa* 5K, *alafu unatoa hizo zingine. Si hiyo ni deal poa?*"

I laugh. "*Na wewe?*" I ask.

"*Kitambo pia.* With this guy who wanted to break up with me but was not telling me. *Nyinyi machali hukuwa complicated sana.*"

"*Machali si* complicated," I say. "Men only want three things."

"*Nini?*"

"Sex, food, and peace."

She looks at me unconvinced. "You know, women think sex keeps a man, but it doesn't. *Ni yeye akupende, na wewe umserve,*" she says finally.

The music stops, and Abby asks if someone is knocking on the door. I get out of bed, head to the living room, and peer through the glass. There's no one. I shuffle the bedroom playlist, and Bobby V comes on: *Slow down. I just wanna get to know you, but don't turn around 'cause that pretty round thing looks good to me… now turn around and bless me with your beauty. You cutie…*

I head to the kitchen and return with two spoons and cups of Frusion yogurt. I hand her the Wild Berry and spoon the Vanilla.

"How does yours taste?" I ask. She offers me a spoonful.

"It's sweeter than mine," I say.

"You can have it," she says, handing me the nearly-empty Wild Berry and taking my barely touched Vanilla. "You're eating so slowly," she teases, draining my cup.

With the yogurt gone, Drake's *Final Fantasy* starts playing on the speakers: *I never really talk about dick that I wanna give you, or places I wanna get to. Neck grab, head grab. Arch back, heart attack, cardiac…* And we're back to kissing. Her mouth finds my ear, nibbling at it as my teeth sink into her neck. We spoon again, but soon I turn her over, placing a pillow under her stomach to support her arched back as I give her all of me.

Her love box makes farting sounds as I go in and out of her and she giggles, embarrassed. Google says it's when air gets caught between your cock and her love box, and it's called queefing. It could be queefing, or maybe it's applause. I suppose we will never know.

I tease her by brushing the tip of my cock against the entrance of her warmth, then thrust it all in without warning. She seems to love it. Sometimes I linger too long, and she throws her hips back, swallowing me into her wetness.

I smack her ass with the force of a fully grown man, the sharp sound of my palm meeting her skin echoing through the room. She doesn't flinch, only lets out a soft moan, which surprises me, so I do it again—and again.

I slow down, lying on top of her, our bodies pressed together. Her eyes are tightly shut, soft moans escaping her lips. I slide my hands into hers, our fingers interlocking, and the sounds we make together are like eating sweet, juicy sugarcane.

"Open your eyes," I groan.

They remain shut.

"Look at me," I plead.

Nothing.

I give her the length of me for a time before falling beside her. She rolls over and looks at me.

"*Uko* sure *wewe si mjaluo?*" she asks.

"*Mbona hutaki kuniangalia?*" I deflect.

"*Oh, ndio nishinde nikikutumia* good morning texts *kila siku.*"

She rests her hand on my waist and lays her head on my chest. There's a hint of skepticism in her eyes, and I wonder why. Then I realize she's noticed the Ventolin inhaler on my bedside table. I glance at it, then back at her.

"*Kama nilikuwa nakufa, ningekufa kitambo.*"

She puts her head on my chest, gently as if it's made of glass.

"*Uliniambia uko na* sisters *wangapi?*"

"*Wawili.*"

"*Na* brothers?"

"*Mimi pekee.*"

"*Uwi.* I fear sisters. *Sasa ukikufa naweza waambia nini? Mimi naweza lia.*" She gets up and pretends to be one of my sisters, "*Woi, kamwana gaitu. Ni kairetu kau gake ka mursik,*" she says in Kikuyu accent before settling back on my chest. "*Uko* in a relationship, *ama kuna mtu anadhani* you're in a relationship *na yeye? Unajua mtu anaweza kuwa* in a relationship *pekee yake,*" she says and laughs.

"There's one who calls every day. *Hata sijui mbona hajacall leo* but *simfeel hivyo.*"

"*Labda* she's saving you."

"*Unamaanisha?*"

"*Haujui madem hufanya hivo. Kuweka chali kama* plan B, in case what they have doesn't work out."

"*Ati?*"

"Probably *wewe ni* plan B *wake.*"

I crease my forehead. "*Na wewe?*"

"There's a guy but *sina* desire. I just see him as a protector." She goes quiet for a while. "Or maybe *nitampatia* chance. Relationship *ni* decision *unamake* to love the other person and you stick by it." She quiets again then continues, "You know a woman can grow to love a man she didn't want before, but a man can never grow to love a woman he doesn't like."

"What happened to *baba mtoto?*" I ask without preamble.

"*Alianza madharau ndogo ndogo.* So I left."

"Does he see the kid?"

"*Akitaka kumuona* we meet in town at a public place."

The music has gone quiet, and she hears knocking on the door again. I get out of bed, head to the living room, and peer through the glass. There's no one. I shuffle the music and return to the bedroom. Pretty Ricky comes on: *Baby grind on me, relax your mind, take your time on me. Let me get deeper, shorty ride on me. Now come and sex me till your body gets weak...*

I get back into bed and lie on my back. She rests her hand on my waist and lays her head on my chest.

"*Unapenda kukula nini? Najua Wakikuyu hawapendi ugali* but *najua kupika mokimo na githeri.*" She goes quiet for a while. "*Naweza pika* but *siwezi fua nguo. Kuna* time after high school *nilikuwa nadate huyu chali. Kwenda kumtembelea nikapata dem mwingine huko akimfulia nguo. Tangu hiyo siku, nilisema sitawahi fulia mwanaume si bwana yangu nguo.*"

"*Mlipigana na huyo dem?*"

"*Hapana. Nilimwambia mimi ni* cousin," she says, giggling.

Jeremih is back with *Birthday Sex,* and we start kissing. Her mouth finds my ear, nibbling it gently as my teeth sink into her neck. She moves down, past my belly button, taking all of me into her mouth.

I shift to take her from behind. She arches her back, drawing me into her wetness. Moans and soft queefs escape her lower lips, her eyes closed in pleasure. I glance at the view, thinking I should capture this moment for later. I grab my phone from the bedside table and open the video function, but it's a challenge to maintain the rhythm while recording. I put the phone away and pick up the tempo.

I wrap her braids around my hand twice for a better grip. It's war now. She moans loudly, and I can't tell if it's from my thrusts or because I'm pulling her braids too hard. The sound of the bed squeaking and my pelvis hitting her back reverberates through the room as I give her my seed for the second time, and fall beside her.

"*Iko kwa miguu zangu.* It's a lot," she complains.

I look at her. Lucky girl. She's gotten the deluxe cock. Most women have not been that lucky.

"Are you sure you don't want to take P2?"

"*Niko* on my safe days. Trust me, I don't want a kid. *Kuna madem hutrap machali na watoto,* but I'm not one of them. *Lazima tuwe* in a relationship and decide on whether to have one."

She goes quiet.

"Kids are just bills, bills, bills… Kids are blessings," she adds, finally.

I just lie there without the energy to move nor speak.

"*Naneed kuoga.* I'm sticky," she says and gets out of bed.

I gather the little energy I have and follow her, deciding that I need to wash my cock.

"This is actually a big house. *Unalalanga kama umewasha stima?*" she asks, in that way women do to make men feel manly about dull things.

I shake my head.

"*Heh, mimi naweza ogopa,*" she says while peeking into my office bedroom. "*Unaweka* double decker *ya watoto kwa hii* room and you're sorted," she says expansively.

I told you I have moments where I catch glimpses of the future, faintly. As we stand there, staring at my office bedroom—which is soon to have a double-decker—I envision us having sex a few times. She starts to realize that no other woman frequents, and gradually, she begins leaving her things behind with each visit. I see her moving in with her son, and I see myself feeling miserable. I don't like that vision at all.

"*Uko tu na* toothbrush *moja. Wewe ni mzuri.* You don't have toothbrushes from other ladies?" she says from the kitchen.

"If a woman leaves something, I usually just throw it away," I say

Abby finds me in the bathroom with the water running on the length of me.

"*Enyewe hii ni nyumba ya* bachelor. *Hiyo* kitchen *iko tu fuaa. Naweza ipanga hadi ushangae,*" she says as I turn off the faucet and realize that my vest has bloodstains on the hem.

"*Iweke kwa maji ikona* jik."

"Will Persil work?"

"*Eh.*"

I put some water and Persil in a bucket and throw it in. The younger me would have thrown it away.

"*Nimeoga tu miguu,*" she says, stepping out of the bathroom. I think, having been inspired by me just washing my cock.

I head to the kitchen and grab the last two cups of Frusion yogurt. I had hidden them for myself, but I've just decided that we should live for the moment. I find Abby seated on the bed, her legs crossed. I hand her the Fruit Cocktail, keeping the Mango & Peach for myself as I sit down on the bed with my feet on the floor.

"*Twende tumalize* movie?"

"*Hapana nataka tuongee. Nitakuja tuwatch* movie *siku ingine,*" she spoons her Fruit Cocktail. "*Ama tutapanga, nisipate mtu huku akiosha nguo.*"

"When was the last time you were with a man?" I ask, my face turning serious. "And be honest?"

"July."

"And when was the last time you got tested for HIV?"

"December, on world AIDS day. What about you?"

"Around August." I spoon my Mango & Peach. "Nobody wants to be sick, you know. Being sick is bad business. You can't work, yet the illness demands money for hospital bills."

"I'm clean," she says, but even as she says it, I know we shall revisit this topic.

"*Kuna* WiFi?" she asks.

"*Kwani,* how do you think everything is playing?" I say, feeling insulted.

I give her the password, and she keys it into her phone. "*Wacha* apps *zikuwe zina* update before *niende.*

Lyttle comes on the speakers: *Let me hold you, girl caress my body. You got me going crazy. You turn me on, turn me on...* while I lie on my back, she sinks her hands on my waist and places her head on my chest.

"We have been fucking all afternoon. *Hata sijui umeenda* rounds ngapi," Abby says, moving her mouth to my ear, and starts nibbling it.

"I'm tired," I say, but she's relentless. She takes me in her mouth for a time, then climbs on top of me. I pick her up with the little energy I have left, and remove her from on top of me. She comes to my lips.

"I want to give you a proper goodbye." We have kissed to the point where our lips are raw and I want no more of it.

"I don't want to do a lousy job," I say with the best intentions.

"So now it's a job?" she says and shows me her back.

I get into the spooning position. "I will do it, *ukiniangalia.*" She looks back at me, but I can't find her love box. I put her in the missionary position. She grabs my cock. She can't find it either.

"*Imejifunga,*" she says while oiling her hand with her saliva and touching herself. Diamond's lyrics in *Kwangwaru* swim in my head: *Weka mate niteleze kama nyoka pangoni...* I put in the length of me, but I want to turn her on her stomach, and take her from the back. "*Itatoka*," she says, but I'm not listening and it spills out. "*Wewe ni mchezo uko nayo sasa*," she says as I fall beside her.

The sun that was filtering through the window has gone, and darkness has taken its place.

"*Time ya kwenda imefika.*"

"*Haulali?*"

"*Nataka*, but my sister will end up taking care of my baby, and she will be mad." She falls back on the cushion. "*Nataka kwenda but sitaki.*"

She gets up. "*Funga macho. Hatujafika place ya kuonana bila nguo.*" She dresses up. I love the way her short purple dress cuts and exposes her thighs. I get out of bed, and we kiss, my hands grabbing her back. "*Unataka turudi tuanze mchezo tena?*" she asks. I shake my head.

I pick up my pants and t-shirt from the floor and grab a gray hoodie from my wardrobe. I look at her; she wants to take photos. I get the ring light from my office bedroom. When she sees it, she wants to doll up. She digs into her handbag and puts on makeup. I open the camera function on my phone. She pouts her lips and throws peace signs in the air. She puts her peace sign close to her chest… then next to her arm… another one on her head. *Women and their peace signs.* I wonder why we don't have world peace yet. She's done with the peace signs, and I send the photos to her WhatsApp.

She looks at the pictures and compliments some of them, then opens the camera function on her phone.

"Let's take a selfie?"

"No," I say flatly.

I take the ring light, and direct it toward the bed.

"*Tu act* movie?"

"*Mambo ya* sextape *sitaki*."

We're ready to go, and she wants the hoodie I'm wearing. "Let me wear it so I smell like you," she says. I rather like this hoodie. I open my laundry basket.

"I'm giving these clothes away. *Unaweza chagua yenye unataka*."

Abby picks a yellow and an orange hoodie. The yellow fits her better, but the orange one has more color. "*Usipatiane hii ya* orange, *nitaikujia*." Even as she's saying this, I know she won't be getting the orange hoodie if she doesn't leave with it today. I get my Deep-Black-Charcoal-Deodorant and spray it on the yellow hoodie she's wearing and we head out to the stage.

"*Unajua sikuwa nadhani utataka* sex?"

"*Ulikuwa unadhani nitataka nini?*"

"*Nilikuwa nadhani tutaongea tu.*"

I laugh. Imagine entering a lion's den thinking it's a chicken coop. But then again, that's the charm of *Bluebeard's Castle.*

"Brian, you've surprised me," she says. "But in a good way."

Remember this girl had my change, about 300 Kenya shillings? *Or has all that sex made you forget?* We had decided we would let her keep the money, but she had to acknowledge she had it first.

We get to the stage; there are no *matatus,* and I don't want to stand there waiting.

"You still have the 300 shillings. *Si* you just take an Uber to town?"

"300 on transport? *Wacha tungojee matatu.*"

A *matatu* stops after a time. I give her a hug and wave goodbye.

I get to the house. I have just had the most intense sex I've had in a while, yet I feel the same. I find this strange. You think you will feel different after having sex, but you don't. It doesn't solve your problems or improve your lifestyle. It's a natural human act, and you just go back to your routines and being who you were, afterward.

Zuchu's *Sukari* is on the TV: *Sukari, nampatia. Ai sugar, sukari. Nampatia… What a beautiful African woman,* I think while watching the video. I look at my phone; I have two texts from Abby.

"Thank you for today. I enjoyed your company."

"Leo utalala kama mtoto mdogo."

"Haha *umenifanyisha* exercise," I reply, avoiding a recap of the sex on text. I switch Zuchu off, piss, wash my hands, brush my teeth, turn off the lights, and go to bed. Google usually plays me rain sounds so I can sleep, but this time it's lights out the moment my head hits the pillow.

Photograph

I WAKE UP on Sunday at around 8:00 p.m. I put on Wiz Khalifa: *We Dem Boyz. Hol' up, hol' up. Hol' up, we dem boys…* I am feeling really good. I rinse my vest in the bucket and put it in the sun. It's moon white, you wouldn't even tell it had bloodstains. I find her hula-hoop earrings on the coffee table and her hairband on the sofa. I pick them up and put them in my drawer as a memento.

I head to Naivas Kasarani, buy sausages, and make my way back to the house. Once there, I fry four of them, an enticing aroma wafting through the air as they hit the hot oil and the sizzle bringing a comforting familiarity. Afterwards, I sit down to enjoy them with four slices of bread and a steaming cup of tea, relishing the simple pleasure of my breakfast.

As I sip my tea, I open my phone and watch the 10-second clip I recorded of her. It's dark and incoherent, a jumbled mix of sounds and images that fails to capture the moment I wanted. I throw the video in the bin. I scroll through WhatsApp; she's posted some of the photos I took on her stories. I finish my breakfast, the sausages now a satisfying warmth in my belly, and pick up where we left off with *Venom* on Netflix. The movie is a welcome distraction, from the unresolved feelings bubbling beneath the surface.

A text comes in from Abby in the afternoon. "Hey Brian… Can you ask Google how to stop someone from running on another one's mind?" She texts from a different number, a detail that pricks at my curiosity. I ask Google, it says it does not understand the question.

This was my problem too when I was in my 20s. Feeling as if I would burst if I didn't tell someone they were on my mind. Now, sitting in my 30s, I realize it's okay for people to be on my mind. My mind is vast, capable of holding countless musings and I don't always need to act on each one.

Monday comes, and I start wondering why I did not use protection. I remind myself that 72 hours have not yet passed since that moment, but the clock is ticking. I could go to Kenyatta National Hospital and get Post Exposure Prophylaxis (PEP) but the prospect of long queues and potential side effects gives me a headache.

Abby said she last had sex in July and got tested on World AIDS Day in December. I ask Google when World AIDS Day is just to fact-check her story. Google tells me it's on December 1st. Dodgy people's stories are always falling apart because they're full of holes. From the time we met, she didn't do anything, but be straight with me, so I don't have reason to doubt her. But still, I am who I am, and I have to cover my bases.

Einstein says a clever man solves a problem, while a wise man avoids it. I could have been a wise man by just using the condoms that were right there in my wardrobe. Today, I will have to be a clever man and hope to be a wise one tomorrow.

I decide to buy an HIV kit and test myself, then send Abby the results, and request her to do the same. If she is as straightforward as she has been with me, she shouldn't have a problem with this.

I step out of the house with my bag at noon. The midday sun is up in the sky, scorching everything in its path. I avoid the chemist next to my flat and walk a bit further to the next one. Inside, I find a well-dressed gentleman and a woman behind the counter. Everything about them suggests they are a couple. I instinctively go to the man.

"Can I have the HIV self-test kit?"

"Oral or blood?"

"Which one is better?"

"They will both give you the same results."

"Give me the oral one."

The woman is directing him to where the kits are, and he returns with one.

"How much?"

"250 shillings."

I am delighted with the price. I pay quickly through M-Pesa, put the kit in my bag, and walk slowly back to my house. I soap up my hands, rinse them, and towel off. I pick up the kit, which is written, *'Chukua selfie'* on it, with a cool hand sign above the words.

I open it, take out the swab, and roll it through my upper and lower gums before dipping it in the liquid provided, as directed on the instructions. Then I start the long wait. "Hey

Google, set a timer for 20 minutes," I say with a shaky voice. There's always anxiety when testing for HIV. I could do this test tomorrow, and I would still feel anxious. The 20 minutes stretch out like a lifetime, but they eventually arrive. One line. I'm negative, and now it's time for the second part of my task.

I text Abby on both numbers: the one she gave me, and the new one from which she recently texted me.

"Hey," I text on the first line.

"Hey."

"Is this your line?"

"I need to tell you something. Respond if this is your line," I text on the new number.

The last thing I want is for the line to be her sister's or someone else's. After a few minutes, I call her but she doesn't pick up. I decide she's busy, and will get back to me when she can. Still, a part of me wonders if she's being dodgy.

I go to buy fruits to just get my head away from things. Abby calls with the old line when I'm buying watermelons. "Hey, I need you to do something for me. I will text you in a few minutes," I tell her. I get to the house and find her texts from her new line waiting for me.

"Yeah, this is still my number."

"Sorry, missed your call."

"What's up?"

I get right to it. "Just took an oral test. I'm negative. Sending you cash. I need you to take one too, so I can stop stressing, or know if I need to take PEP. Is that cool?" I share an image of my negative result.

"Okay, no problem." I find her incredibly attractive after this text comes in.

I send her the cash, plus extra for the trouble.

"But PEP is advised to be taken within 24 hrs after sexual intercourse. But I'll send you my results, *ndiyo uache* stress."

"It's actually within 72 hours," I text back. Believe me, I have done extensive research on this.

"*Lakini sijai ona* Brayo, who is this cautious… you should change your name," she says with laughing emojis.

45 minutes later, her text comes in. One line—she's negative too. I glance at her fingers in the photo. Her nails are still purple, just as they were on Saturday. I notice her surroundings; the tiles in the background tell me she took the test in her job's washrooms. The same washrooms I've seen before while at the barbershop.

She couldn't have doctored the results or gotten someone else to take the test for her. She wouldn't have thought that far ahead in such a short amount of time. I wouldn't have either. If I had, I would have bought the kits after the first round, and we could have tested together. Then I might have been somewhat of a wise man instead of just a clever one.

I open my phone to more of Abby's texts.

"After three months we'll take the test again."

"Do you trust my results, or you went ahead and took the PEP?"

"Are you home?"

I look at the last text. I know I now have the kind of clearance where I could tell her to clock out of work early, and come over, and she would. I could really use the tightness between her legs, but that comes with its own expectations and promises, so I answer the question that needs answering.

"I trust them," I text back.

I sit down and ask myself what those expectations and promises would look like. The vision flashes in front of me again—her and her son living with me, me doing things out of obligation, and her making most of her decisions with her son in mind. I don't like that vision at all.

We could be friends, or friends with benefits, but that's toxic too, especially when one person wants more. You shouldn't spend large amounts of time with someone who wants you in that way if you don't see yourself with them in the foreseeable future.

The sun rises and sets on Tuesday and Wednesday. Good morning texts go unanswered. She texts again on Wednesday evening.

"Hey, how are you? You know, I wanna believe you're busy or contemplating what happened between us. Things happened so fast, you know. What have you been up to?"

"Hey, I'm good. I'm just silent because I don't want to give you false hope."

"Okay. Out of curiosity, did I say or do anything wrong that made you feel that way?"

"No, no. You were actually pretty cool."

"Alright. I kinda liked you, but you know, the feeling has to be mutual in order for it to work. I respect your decision. Thank you."

I want to tell her to come over, and we can make it work. The decision feels hard, but I know I have to make it. It's an easier decision to make now compared to the one I'd have to make later, after our lives are intertwined together and there's more at stake.

I wake up on Thursday feeling down and out. After breakfast, I put on some soft music and sit at my desk. Ed Sheeran's *Photograph* comes on: *Loving can hurt. Loving can hurt sometimes, but it's the only thing that I know.* I find myself crying, convulsing violently to the lyrics. *When it gets hard, you know it can get hard sometimes. It is the only thing that makes us feel alive...* I cry at my flaws, at our expectations, and at what we both thought could be but never will, as Ed Sheeran's *Photograph* plays on and on.

Surviving Henry

Meeting him, you wouldn't have been able to tell he was a monster. That's the thing about predators: they are uncanny in their camouflage. Henry was all smiles and common courtesy. He was of average height, well-kempt, easy to like, and the one thing that had me sitting across from him was that he was the Business Manager in the company where I had applied for a job.

There was something else about Henry—he had a fruity demeanor. It was the way he walked with a bounce in his step, like some model on a runaway, or the way he used his hands a little too much when talking.

What another man did in private was not my concern, I decided. Besides, we'd be meeting in office corridors, far removed from carnal needs and raw sexual charge. I was wrong about this—and about a lot more.

I sat across from him and took him in. He was dressed in a maroon shirt and gray denim jeans. He twirled the straw in his glass of pineapple juice and puckered his lips around the tip to sip the pale yellow liquid. With a stroke of his pen, he could change my luck. I knew it, and he did too.

"As I was saying, I am very passionate about storytelling," I repeated.

"Drew," he shortened my name with a twang, as if giving it a long kiss with his puckered lips. "Work is for the office; this is a bar and lounge, where we eat, drink, and make merry," he added, picking up a chicken lollipop from his plate. It disappeared into his mouth, and only a clean bone emerged, which he later shredded before dropping it onto a separate plate already piled with shredded bones. "Gawd! The marrow is everything," he remarked.

Fresh out of university, green and naive, I was more fascinated than wary of his antics. I adjusted my blue suit, which was a size bigger than me, nibbled on a chicken lollipop, and took a sip of my passion juice. I was passionate about storytelling after all.

"Look at the swinging hips on that one," he said, pointing to a waitress in a black mini-dress across the lounge who was all legs. It was an attempt at guy talk which only made me uncomfortable. "You know what the problem with you is?" he asked after shredding another chicken bone, "You're too sober," he answered his own question. "Bring us two Screwdriver cocktails," he added after calling the waitress who was all legs.

I'd had a drink before—cheap lagers that only gave me a buzz. The Screwdriver, though, made me tipsy after just three sips. And it was a tall glass. "I don't think I can finish this," I admitted.

"5,000 shillings if you can make it halfway," he teased, placing the money on the table.

It all felt strange, but money is money, and by the end of the evening, I had 10,000 Kenya shillings in my pocket. We made our way to the basement parking lot, where his white Audi A4 beeped and the doors unlocked.

"Let's sit at the back for a while so the booze in our heads clears," Henry suggested. I could barely walk, even though I'd only had one Screwdriver, but he seemed sober despite drinking three.

"We should probably get an Uber," I suggested.

"Forget Ubers. I drive an Audi, and you want to jump into a cramped Passo? Gawd! Andrew, have some class," he said while opening the back left door for me. "After you, Boss," he remarked before going around and sitting on my right side.

He handed me a bottle of water and began talking about the company, and how bright the future was for people who were smart and knew how to follow instructions.

During his glib, he seemed to be leaning closer and closer to me. "Gawd! You're so tall and yellow, yellow," he groaned. Thinking he might be blacking out, I prepared to catch him. Only, we came face to face and his lips grabbed mine.

I pulled back immediately. "Don't be like that, Drew," he slurred. "Do you want the job or not?" he asked, squeezing my bicep.

I opened the door and staggered out of the basement parking lot. I walked for quite a while, my mind blank, before realizing I had 10,000 shillings in my pocket and called an Uber. Surprisingly, it was a Passo that showed up.

As I was driven to my bedsitter in Roysambu, my mind was awash with thoughts. I was a hot-blooded male who was attracted to women and only women. What made Henry think he could come onto me like that? Was it the booze? Or was this his usual behavior? One thing was clear in my mind: I would rather stay in my situation a hundred lifetimes and then some, than crawl into bed with him for all the riches in the world.

The Internship

Despite everything, i landed an internship at the company. No, not through the back door—that was out of the question. After several rounds of interviews, I was finally sent a contract. You see, just like there are terrible people in this world who try to take advantage of others, there are also good people who believe in helping others advance on merit, not by how loose their moral compass might be.

So there I was, working under Henry. We never talked about that evening—it never came up, not once. It had happened three months ago, but it felt like a lifetime ago.

I'd decided to leave the past where it belonged, though I did make a point to M-Pesa him back the 10,000 Kenya shillings he'd given me after my first salary was credited into my account.

We were cordial for the first six months. However, I'd be remiss to jump straight to the dynamics of our working relationship without mentioning the company's culture. It seemed that new hires were the latest sex toys for upper management. If you looked around and saw a beautiful girl or a handsome man, you could almost bet they were involved with one of the heads.

I'd picked up on this one Friday evening. We often found ourselves in a nearby bar, having a drink or two as we wound down the week. Norah, one of my colleagues, approached me. She had brown skin, was slender, and wore a short black skirt, platform heels, purple stockings, and braids, that gave her a Harley Quinn-meets-night-nurse vibe. In her hand was a pink drink, bubbling just like her personality.

"Soooo, who's your blesser?" Norah asked, glancing at the honchos in the room: Henry, the CEO, the Creative Director, and the Chief Operational and Financial Officers.

"What do you mean?" I replied, clueless, as I unbuttoned my coat—a well fitted, pale brown number I'd just bought and was hoping would catch some attention.

"I mean, who's calling your tuuune…. you know, from the saying, 'he who pays the piper calls the tuuune,'" she added, and giggled after seeing the confusion on my face.

"I applied and got an internship on merit," I finally replied.

"Oh, you're actually telling the truth," she said, sobering up momentarily, and looked at me with shock, as if I were from another planet.

"He used to call the tuuune," she said, glancing at the Creative Director, a stocky clean-cut man pouring Jameson onto his glass. "Until he found a tighter cuuunt, I suppose," Norah added bitterly, pointing a purple-manicured nail at a light-skinned girl sitting beside him. The girl was a recent hire who'd just been confirmed as the Account Manager.

For the rest of that night, Norah went on to tell me what I hadn't needed to know, glancing around the room and revealing everyone's blessers. I was astonished by some of the men Henry was involved with—simultaneously, no less. Macho men with girlfriends and wives, men who often set the standard for masculinity among their friends.

I wanted to cry and laugh at the same time, but when it came down to it, it seemed what most people truly worshiped was money. Money meant you could move to a better neighborhood, drive a nice car, and wear trendy clothes. Money meant the latest iPhone and adoration from the congregation of everyone else who worshiped on the same altar.

I resolved to keep my dignity, even though it felt like the hardest thing to do in a place that was rotting from the inside out.

As the night wore on, Norah shifted from bitterness to tears, asking how she could win him back and regretting confiding in me. "Don't tell anyone else what I told you, prooomise?" she whimpered. As far as I could tell, there was no one to tell—there was no secret that everyone already knew.

Lights Out

AT THE SIX-MONTH MARK, the tension between Henry and me started rising. He would come into the office, say hello to everyone, and skip me. Sometimes, he'd bring treats for everyone—except me. He constantly criticized my work, even when everyone else in my department only had positive feedback.

I found it childish. Life is strange that way; when someone takes a stance against you, it's almost instinctual to take the opposite. It's as if that's what keeps this blue marble rotating on its axis. So, I took the high road every time he took the low one.

"You'll have to redo this report. It reeks of amateur hour," Henry barked one morning, as he often did.

"No problem," I replied, returning to my desk.

It was quite amusing how he targeted me rather than the work. The report had already been approved by the client in a recent status meeting that he hadn't attended, and I knew he hadn't even looked at it. I sat down, and changed the theme, and waited until he asked for it again.

"It's no good," he said. "Try picking up the pace—slightly faster than a tortoise this time," he added.

My internship review was just around the corner, and office gossip hinted that he was trying to get me fired for incompetence. But, truthfully, he didn't need a reason. Once he was bored with a subordinate, he'd simply whisper to his circle of cutthroats and have them dismissed on whatever flimsy grounds they dreamed up during their board meetings—often held in bars.

I decided to get ahead of things by talking to him directly. In my mind, I believed he'd listen to reason. On a Wednesday evening, I found myself back at the bar and lounge where this had all started, seated across from him with a lager in my hand and a Screwdriver in his.

"You know, I have nothing against you, Henry," I began. "You don't need to feel threatened by me."

"I have nothing against you," he replied, and I raised an eyebrow. "Believe it or not, Drew," he continued with a slight twang before his lips returned to his straw momentarily, "I want you to thrive in this company."

"And what about…"

"Water under the bridge," he cut me off. "How about I get you a drink as a sign of our truce?" He got up and went over the counter. He came back with a shot-glass. Inside was what looked like the Screwdriver he'd been drinking. "See? I know you're a lightweight, so I got you the right size."

"Thank you," I said, raising my glass, a bit frustrated with myself for turning nothing into something, as we made a toast to new beginnings.

I don't remember when the lights went out, and everything faded to black. But I knew, deep down, that it had something to do with the drink Henry had given me.

Part of the Circle

I WOKE UP in an Airbnb in Kilimani the next morning. At first, I didn't know where I was. My throat was parched, and there was discomfort in my anus. I saw the lube, then I saw the note on the bedside table: *Everything has been paid for. You can take an off day today.* And I immediately knew what Henry had done.

I took a scalding hot shower as I tried to process what had happened. Every part of my body felt filthy. While I was scrubbing myself, I realized Henry had multiple partners and he probably didn't use protection with any of them. After the shower, I dressed up, got an Uber, and rushed to AAR.

"You know, if you're really concerned about your sexual health, you should come with your girlfriend. It helps build trust," the doctor said, oblivious of my situation. She prescribed PEP (Post-Exposure Prophylaxis) that I was to take for 28 days.

The next day, I returned to the office with a black hoodie pulled over my head and dark sunglasses shielding my eyes. I didn't want the world to see my shame. I sat at my desk and opened up my laptop, fighting a wave of nausea that rose every so often, threatening to bring up the samosa and tea I'd forced down that morning.

"Is everything okay?" Norah asked. She looked as worn out as I felt, her floral shirt-dress wrinkled and in desperate need of an iron, with eye bags so heavy not even makeup could cover them. She looked as though she'd spent the previous night looking for something at the bottom of a wine glass, going from bottle to bottle, and after the sun came up, it was still nowhere to be found.

"A bit of nausea, but I'll be fine," I replied. She gave me a familiar sheepish look—a look that said, *Remember not to tell anyone my dirty little secret.*

I turned back to my laptop and found an email summoning me to HR. I thought Henry had finally pulled the plug, and I was about to be out on my ass. Instead, Carolina, the Head of HR—a tall black woman who wore blonde wigs and whose appetites were rumored to be similar to Henry's—was not only confirming me but promoting me to Head of Client Service, with a salary package five times what I'd been earning. Say what you will about money but it has a way of dulling the sting, albeit momentarily.

In hindsight, I should have rejected the offer and ran as far as I could from that place. But part of me felt it was the least Henry could do, and the package seemed like a small price to pay for what I had endured.

The end of the month was around the corner, and my promotion was set to start effective immediately. I had never seen so many zeros in my bank account statement. I could take a mortgage, put a down payment on a car, take a vacation, no, vacations.

Now, I'd never been one for flashy displays, but the comfort and ease that money brought with it opened up a Pandora's box I never knew existed within me. The second-hand clothes were quickly replaced by Woolworths, LC Waikiki, and Mr. Price. I moved out of my bedsitter in Roysambu to a two-bedroom house in South B and put a down payment on a BMW 116i which I would finish paying with bank financing within a year. It sounded like a short period, but those 12 months ended up being some of the longest days of my life.

After I was properly tethered to the yoke of earthly possessions, Henry came knocking for his pound of flesh, and I finally understood the saying: there's no such thing as a free lunch. The first time I had sex with him sober, I cried. You don't want to see a grown man crying. His tears mix with mucus while he wipes them away with the back of his hand, but the downpour won't stop, and the hiccups keep coming to confirm to you that you are truly at rock bottom.

For our next sessions, I downed three shots of vodka just to get through the foreplay. Yes, there was foreplay. Henry was paying premium fees and he would settle for nothing less than the full experience. I had to take three more shots to undress and another three to get through the act. I was on a steady prescription of PEP, to the point I barely felt its side effects anymore.

Introductions to the circle of cutthroats, who were basically the entire upper management except for two or three people who still had to play the game of appearances, followed swiftly. *I was one of them now,* I thought, *just as filthy as they were.*

I sat with them in high-end bars, restaurants, and hotels around the city, watching them drink, do drugs, and gossip. On and on they went about their conquests; about who was a good lay, who they were promoting, and who needed to get laid off because they had gotten too fat, too lazy, or too… whatever their drug-fueled paranoia concocted. "Cheer up, Andrew," the Creative Director said to me one evening, "It's only a matter of time before you'll be robbing the cradle too."

Ironically, it was the vodka that saved me. I spiraled into alcoholism, and my work began to suffer—eventually, not even Henry could cover for me. After about a year at the company I staggered into the office one fine morning, well, late morning, close to noon—definitely not fine. I was operating on autopilot. Unthinking, unfeeling, inhuman. I opened my work email and there it was, a dismissal letter from Carolina on the grounds of gross misconduct.

I rose from my desk, laughing, and walked to the reception and lifts still laughing. I found it amusing that I was being fired for being drunk. A coping mechanism I had acquired from the true misconduct that was happening in the organization, and for the first time in a long while, I felt human again.

Free Fall

For someone who was being paid a hefty sum—to the tune of 500,000 Kenya shillings a month, my account was empty. You'd be astonished at how quickly the high life gobbles up money. There's the gym and country club membership you rarely use, the motorbike you never ride, nights spent in five-star hotels because you spotted a gecko in your house—the list of wastefulness is endless.

Selling the BMW, the motorbike, and every other frivolous purchase was the easy part. Moving from South B to a one-bedroom house in Ngong was manageable. The hard part was accepting that I had an alcohol problem and needed help.

In a year or so, I drank through most of my money. Eventually, I couldn't make rent and got kicked out of the Ngong house.

I ended up in run-down lodgings. I remember bumping into Henry in downtown CBD, where I had resorted to hanging out because of the availability of cheap liquors and accommodation, and he almost couldn't recognize me. He had a young man in the passenger's seat of his Audi. They were there for a brand campaign and I felt the sting that Norah had felt of being replaced.

"I guess I will see you around," he said, in that dismissive way people do when they're certain they never want to see you again. I knew I'd be a juicy topic in their circle of cutthroats. I knew it would also be a relief to them. Their biggest worry was getting sued, and their gravy train coming to an abrupt stop. In my state, I wouldn't harm a fly, let alone get to Henry. That was the moment I resolved to rise from rock bottom.

Retribution

I SIGNED UP for Alcoholics Anonymous at All Saints Cathedral in Nairobi-CBD and began attending meetings religiously. To keep busy, I took up delivery services, initially on foot and later on a hired electric bicycle around the city. I moved to a bedsitter in Waruku, and when I wasn't making deliveries, I was at a cyber café sending out CVs.

I questioned my choices and sanity as I cycled through the city, delivering pizzas, burgers, and parcels to people oblivious to my struggles, while waiting for feedback from the organizations I applied to that never seemed to come.

However, there were also moments of calm, where I reminded myself to believe and push forward, confident that what I wanted would eventually come. After eight months it finally did; a middle management job at a company I had been eyeing.

The culture was collaborative, and hiring and promotions were based on merit. In the first six months, I was anxious, never trusting the tea and coffee provided at the office, opting instead for bottled water from the supermarket, afraid someone would spike my drink or tap me on the shoulder out of the blue because the piper had been paying and the time had come for me to sing their tune. But that day never arrived, and I slowly began to relax.

One fine morning, I received news that shook me. I had just moved into a two-bedroom apartment in Mountain View and completed the payment on my Toyota Prius. Sitting at my desk, I had just sent some money to my grandmother back in the village. I was sipping porridge and eating *nduma*, my skin glistening with good health. "That Business Head from that advertising company is being sued for sexual misconduct," one of my colleagues remarked.

I immediately searched for Henry online. The news was filled with stories about him drugging an ambassador's son at a concert, stirring up a hornet's nest, and now, his victims were coming out of the woodwork in droves, demanding justice.

"Looks like the judge is really going to throw the book at him," my colleague added.

"The haves must be touched for there to be real progress in this city," another shrugged.

Around lunch hour, I silently got into my Prius, drove to Milimani Law Courts, and submitted my statement. On my way back to the office, I saw someone familiar staggering around the bars scattered across Westlands around Mpaka Rd. "Norah," I called, and she looked at me. She hesitated before walking towards me.

She was all bones, in torn clothes, and missing teeth. "Andrew, is that you?" she asked, her face lighting up. "Give me 50 shillings for a drink," she added.

"Get in the car, let's talk," I said. It turned out she had received the same letter I did, a year after I left, and she had recently been evicted from her house.

"I need a drink," she insisted, so I stopped at a Wines and Spirits and bought her a bottle of wine and she hummed back to life. Like me, her family was upcountry, and she had no other means of help besides the streets. The streets would help her all the way to the grave, I knew.

I called my workplace and told them I had an emergency and wouldn't be able to come in the afternoon. My reporting manager easily consented—it was the least he could do after all the good work I had been putting in.

"You're going to stay with me," I told Norah, "but on one condition. You'll attend Alcoholics Anonymous without fail, and you'll manage the supermarket I'm setting up in Waruku." She nodded skeptically. I was content with that; I would draw it out until it became a yes and soon, a 'hell-yes'. Once she was back on her feet, she'd find her own job, and we'd go our separate ways. But we make plans, and God laughs—don't we?

In the months that followed, I watched Norah progress from drinking a bottle of wine a day to half a bottle, then to a glass, and finally to drinking only on weekends. We went to the hospital for a thorough checkup and were relieved to receive negative results. Her teeth were fixed, she started eating regularly, and the weight returned to her bones. There she was again—the bubbly Norah I'd always known, dressed in her colorful skirts, stockings, and dresses, on which I suspected she spent most of her salary.

Around that time, I began experiencing slumps that started affecting my work, leading me to take a 30-day leave. I would sit on the couch all day, staring wide-eyed at the TV without really seeing it. *"You've climbed out of the trenches, and now you want to go right back?"* I would tell myself, but for some reason, my will to do something about it seemed to be non-existent.

"You're grieving Henry," Norah said one evening after returning from the supermarket. She had just made supper, and my plate was untouched. I raised an eyebrow and shook my head, lacking the energy to say the, "Hell no!" I wanted to shout.

"It's okay," she said, climbing onto the couch and cuddling me. It wasn't the first time she'd done it. The first time, I felt as though I were consoling a colleague, but over time, I found myself stealing glances, only to meet her big brown eyes, and infectious smile. Now, there was an undeniable spark between us. "I've had to grieve for all of my oppressors leaving me, and when I couldn't take it anymore, I'd reach for a glass of wine. Perhaps we should both try therapy," she added.

Our therapist, a plump, jovial woman Norah had found, held both our hands and guided us toward recovery—or at least, a semblance of it. Something that bothered me was how someone could knowingly harm another human being and how a part of me still felt that they deserved mercy. "All our pain is an opportunity for us to reach within and come out the other end as better people. You cannot control what others do; you can only control what you do," she said, and I have carried this tidbit around like a warm hug.

I returned to work and slowly emerged from my slump. Norah stopped drinking altogether and is completely focused on the supermarket. I'm impressed everyday by the plans she has for it. We continue to keep each other accountable. We need to be even more careful now that we are expecting a child. We need to ensure they never feel trapped enough to make the same unfortunate choices we made.

Yes, we responded to the spark. I was stealing glances, our eyes met, our lips found each other, and the rest as they say, is diapers, baby formula, and being woken up in the wee hours of the night.

Oh, you're wondering what happened to Henry? The judge really did throw the book at him—98 years, which loosely translates to life in prison. Harsh! Don't drop the soap, sir. Haha. I also heard the company he worked for got new management, and the circle of cutthroats is being uprooted one by one, root and stem. Yes, karma is slow, but it always arrives.

The Girl With A Stalker

I know, I know, I know there is someone following me. He has been following me for months. I quicken my steps and cross Moi Avenue, and join throngs of people at the Kenya National Archives. I can hear his footsteps, heavy behind me. If I focus hard enough, I can see his brown leather shoes and smell the citrus in his Sauvage perfume. I wipe sweat from my brow with the back of my hand, tighten the grip on my handbag and pick up my pace, my heart beating faster now. *What does he want with me?*

I join Ronald Ngala Street and begin weighing my options; I could start running, but he is faster than me. I could face him, let him know I am not the coward he thinks I am, or I could go to the authorities. The third option is out of the question. *How do I tell the police that the person who has been following me is my ex-boyfriend and my sister's husband?*

I decide to go with the second option. I slow down; he is almost brushing my navy blue blazer and beige trousers, and his breath is misting my ear. I come to a screeching halt and turn around, "Leave me alone!" I bark. A strange man in a gray suit and two college girls, one in blue ripped jeans and the other in a purple mini-skirt look at me eerily before disappearing into the sea of people on Ronald Ngala Street.

I lean on the wall opposite the entrance of Naivas Supermarket and breathe out a sigh. Every single eyeball is fixated on me, screaming, "Look at that crazy woman." But I know he is around here somewhere, watching me, following me, driving me up the wall. I know, I know, I know.

I get up from my leaning position and continue walking towards Railways Bus Station. My phone rings as I approach the stage. I check the caller ID. It's my sister, Ivy. I ignore her and put it back in my handbag. I enter a minibus heading to Langata, and sit next to a lean man in a black sweater, khaki trousers, and black loafers. He has one of those common faces that are neither ugly nor attractive. I could fuck him on a bad day, and today has been horrible. Another day of tarmacking with nothing to show for it.

"*Pesa mkononi*," the *makanga* sings as he gets to our seat. My seatmate hands him 100 Kenya shillings.

"*Wawili?*" he asks.

The lean man raises one finger and the *makanga* gives him back 50 shillings. My jaw tightens. *What happened to chivalry?* I wonder as I dig into my big wine-red handbag and start looking for my wallet. I rummage through a make-up kit, Nana Darkoa's book *The Sex Lives of African Women*, and a bottle of tablets I haven't touched in months before I find my wallet and pay my fare.

After the *makanga* leaves our seat, I look at the lean man. His gaze is turned to the window. I tap him softly on the shoulder. "Please *fungua dirisha*," I say with my most demure voice in an attempt to start a conversation.

He struggles with the window for a moment before it finally opens. I wait for him to ask my name, my phone number, or something, but he goes back to staring out the window as a soft breeze kisses my skin, making my nipples poke my orange blouse. He is obviously not the strongest, nor the most confident man in the world, but I still want him to talk to me. Maybe his dick could take some of my misery away.

The distractions of my carnal needs almost make me forget about my stalker ex. *What if he followed me into the matatu?* I start looking around the minibus. I see his brown leather shoes peeking from the back seat. My heart starts beating faster and faster. I get up and race toward his seat.

"Leave me the hell alone!" I roar.

Everyone in the *matatu* goes quiet and stares at me as if I am crazy. My heart rate slows down and I feel lightheaded before the mist clears and I am able to see what is in front of me—a frightened schoolboy with a brown leather bag on the floor. I walk back to my seat, embarrassed. My seatmate gets up slowly and moves to another seat.

I bury my face in Nana Darkoa's book and shut out the world. I lift my head as the *matatu* comes to a stop at Carnivore stage. I realize with chagrin that no one dared to sit next to me, not even new passengers. It's as if they could see the warning on the other passengers' faces and hear their thoughts. *"Don't sit next to her, she's not all there."*

THE SUN IS beginning to go down when I get off the minibus. I put the book in my handbag, look right, left and right again before crossing the road and entering our estate's main gate. It's full of two-storey houses with terra-cotta colored clay roof tiles. Some are well taken care of, while others are splitting at the seams, with the paint having been replaced by mud and rust devouring their gates.

I walk for a minute or two before I get to our three bedroom house—it's one of the decent ones in the neighborhood. My mom, who is now retired, always brags about how she saved up money from her government job as a secretary and bought the house. I push open our light blue gate to find her Toyota Corolla parked outside. As I approach the door, I hear laughter and then I see familiar shoes at the door. My sister and her mannerless son, Liam, are visiting.

I stop for a second and wonder if I should turn around and go to a nearby restaurant. I could nurse a drink and read my book until they leave, but I decide that this is my house too. Besides it could be worse, Ken's Subaru Forester could be parked next to my mom's Toyota Corolla. I slip out of my orange low heel sandals, breathe a heavy sigh and press the doorbell.

"Hello, Ivy, so good to see you," I chirp, after my sister opens the door. She is in an African print dera, and even with its loose, flowing fabric, her hourglass figure is still visible.

"Hi Sofia, it's been so long," she says as she throws herself towards me, almost knocking me down with a hug. My hands remain firmly at my sides as she wraps hers tightly around me.

After I enter the living room, my mom comes from the kitchen in her headgear, apron, leso, and slippers, says hello, and then disappears back. I sit on the gray three-seater sofa next to the door, sink my feet in the cream carpet and try to pretend that everything is okay.

Ivy sits next to me and my body stirs. "I was just telling mom that Ken and I are thinking of moving houses. You are in Real Estate, maybe you could help us?" she says and pauses, giving her son a piercing look after realizing he hasn't said hello to me.

Liam is wearing a yellow Mickey Mouse shirt and shorts. He is lounging on one of the one-seater sofas, his legs dangling over the armrest while watching TV.

"Hi, Sofia," he says eventually before sticking his face back to *SpongeBob.* I suppose the expensive private school he attends hasn't bothered teaching him, that your sister's mother is your aunt.

"You're moving again," I say, trying to feign interest while glancing at *SpongeBob*. I'm surprised my mom allowed the TV to be switched from Joel Osteen and T.D. Jakes on Family TV to Nickelodeon.

"Driving to the shops is exhausting. I need a house that is within walking distance of the mall. Preferably one with a playroom for Liam," Ivy says.

Liam glances away from *SpongeBob* and looks at us—*eavesdropping little creature.* I wonder silently why a five-year-old needs a playroom when he can't tell the difference between his aunt and his agemates.

"Will you help us?" Ivy asks, after sensing my hesitation, as my mom reappears from the kitchen to pick the potatoes she'd been peeling in the living room.

Your husband was following me again, I want to tell my sister. "I... I... I will see what I can do," I say instead after remembering how the last conversation went. Knowing her, she has already found a house and this is her way of rubbing it in. This is her way of telling me, *"Look at how I'm moving up in life, while you're still at the same place I left you."*

"Sofia, I need help in the kitchen," my mom says after sensing I'm on the verge of opening a can of worms. "I don't want your sister to have to cook tonight," she adds.

"Include Ken too," Ivy says. "He's coming to pick us up later." My skin crawls at the mention of that name and tension in the room intensifies. Ivy gets up from beside me, goes to Liam, and distracts herself by running her fingers through his thick, dark afro. It is the one thing we have in common: Good hair.

"Ouch, you're hurting me," Liam complains. *She'd have to buy him the entire Disney World for him to allow her to touch his hair,* I think, and grin while getting up, wearing flip-flops and clapping them on the cold hard tiles, past the water dispenser as I join my mom in the kitchen.

You would think she is cooking for an army. There is rice on one burner, steamed spinach on another, goat ribs on the third, and she's frying chips for Liam on the fourth. She is doing all these while kneading dough to make *chapatis.*

"Fry the beans with coconut milk like you usually do, and make a fruit salad," she demands.

"Ken was following me today," I begin to tell her but stop myself and grab a clean *sufuria* instead. I take the rice, which is already done, off the burner and start making my bean stew.

"I haven't seen you in church in a while?" my mom mumbles into her dough and from the corner of my eye, I can see the concern etched in the creases on her face, a reminder that she'll be turning 60 soon.

The sufuria sizzles as I fry onions with garlic, green pepper, and tomatoes. I add salt and seasoning, then stir in half a cup of coconut milk. After pouring the already cooked beans into the *sufuria,* I stir the mixture again and cover it with a lid to let the stew cook. As my mom starts rolling *chapatis* and placing them on the pan that has replaced the pot of steamed spinach.

"You could join your sister in praise and worship. You know she was made the lead singer?" she starts talking again after realizing I was not planning on responding to her question. "You never know, you might find a man too. A God-fearing man is the best kind of man," she says while adding another *chapati* on top of the previous ones.

I have tried church and neither the men nor the worship worked for me but because religion gives her peace, happiness, and a sense of purpose, my mom thinks it will do the same for me, so she pushes it down my throat every chance she gets. It's selfish.

"I will come one of these days," I say to kill the conversation while picking a fresh tray and begin dicing the pawpaw, pineapple, watermelon, and bananas. I then add three teaspoons of honey and stir the mixture together.

"You could start this Sunday. There is a Boys Brigade event and Liam will be performing," she says while applying oil to her *chapatis* as I lift the lid on my beans and add coriander leaves.

I mutter, "Mmh", "Okay", or "Eh". I am not sure. My heart beats faster again. I feel lightheaded after hearing the voice of the man who has been following me, in the living room.

I MET KEN shortly after I started working. I was in my mid-20s, vibrant with the glow of youth and a paycheck. He came to our Real Estate agency at Hurlingham looking for a house.

My boss assigned him to me. Some men can sometimes be touchy and obnoxious in private, so I always insisted on bringing a colleague when giving property tours.

My colleague was busy on this particular day, so I asked my sister, Ivy, who is a year younger than me, to tag along to the five-bedroom luxury Villa in Kileleshwa. With our brown complexion, soft shoulders, small waists, and similar height, people often mistake us for twins. If you were to put us side by side, you could have said we were both pretty, but for every five compliments, three belonged to my sister. There was no rift between us—in fact, we were friends who shared almost everything with each other.

I remember Ivy saying Ken was nerdy and indecisive. "I wouldn't last 30 minutes with such a man," she said while we were in the American-style kitchen of the villa, and Ken had gone to look at the pool again. "But someone is going to live with him for a lifetime. Can you imagine?"

"What is it they say about one man's poison?" I replied, feeling the smoothness of the marble countertop and glancing at the yellow star-shaped light fixtures on the ceiling.

"Is another woman's meat," Ivy said, and we giggled.

Ken was five years older than me, in his second job as a Software Engineer. He drove a red Subaru Forester and he had a taste for the finer things in life. Despite that, he was nervous. He kept repeating questions already answered. "Just double-checking; you can never be too sure," he kept saying. Despite his nervousness, he was good-looking—

wide-chested, dark-skinned and tall. I am 5'5", so every guy might seem tall to me, but, let's say he was of average height, someone you could lose in a crowd. His fashion sense was lacking; he wore a black-and-white checked shirt with black jeans and brown leather shoes, but that was something I could fix.

"So you said the pool is heated," Ken asked again while joining us in the kitchen.

"It is, and you can switch off the heater anytime to save electricity," I repeated.

"Just double-checking; you can never be too sure."

A month after Ken purchased the villa, we were together in that pool, christening it, and in no time, he asked me to be his girlfriend, and I accepted.

I would spend most of my weekends in his villa, often with my sister. Sometimes my sister would get there before me while I was finishing up work, and I would find her in the living room, with the fireplace crackling, chatting and laughing with Ken on the couch. I never thought much of it until the day I got to the office and was summoned to the Human Resources office.

The HR lady, in a sagging taupe frock with her glasses lowered to the tip of her nose—almost falling above her upper lip, where a thin coat of a mustache clung—told me in a calm and firm voice they had obtained evidence I was seducing clients and sleeping with them for favors. Ken's name came up a couple of times, followed by other names and a dismissal letter.

I kept asking myself who could have done this to me. I fell into depression for days and stopped visiting Ken for a while because I didn't want to burden him with my troubles. At this time, I noticed with curiosity that my sister was growing rounder each day and wearing baggy clothes to cover it up.

I came back from tarmacking one day and found her sitting next to Ken in our living room. I remember that day well because it was supposed to be our one-year anniversary, and I was planning to break the distance and the silence by spending time with him that weekend. But there he was, in our living room with my sister—fingers intertwined—across from my mother, announcing they were pregnant and planning to get married. I lost it. I screamed and kicked and screamed some more.

Before I knew it, I was strapped on a stretcher, speeding to the hospital in an ambulance. When I arrived, I was sedated and given a cocktail of pills after being diagnosed with a severe case of denial, bordering on amnesia. As if that was not enough, Ken started following me everywhere.

"Sofia, are you listening to me? I said turn off the burner; the beans are burning." I hear my mom saying after my heart rate slows down and the mist clears.

"Take this to Liam," she adds, while turning off the burner herself and handing me a bowl full of fries.

I take the bowl and my flip-flops clap the floor as I walk toward the living room. Ken gets up as soon as he sees me.

"Hi, Sofia," he says while extending his hand to greet me.

I want to hold him by his collar and shout, "Stop stalking me you son of a bitch!" But instead, I mumble a hello back and shake his hand. He has changed into a dapper blue suit, maroon tie, and matching socks, but I can still smell the citrus notes of his Sauvage perfume.

"Glad to see you," he says, flashing a nervous smile.

"Let me help Mom serve the food," my sister says, while getting up and sprinting to the kitchen.

I know his brown leather shoes are outside. I make my way to the main door and turn the lock. There is another car parked outside the compound—A mercury gray Nissan Outlander with alloy rims. I glance at the doorstep and see my low-heel sandals, my mom's black *Bata-ngomas*, Ivy's pink crocs, Liam's Super Mario sneakers, and maroon loafers I don't recognize, all scattered haphazardly as if everyone rushed in.

I lock the door and get back to the living room, feeling confused. Ken is seated uneasily on the edge of the sofa, while Liam is still slouched in his seat with his bowl of food, watching *SpongeBob*. "There is no ketchup on these fries," he complains, getting up from his position and placing the bowl on the brown table, before pushing it even further. It's a miracle it doesn't fall off the table.

I stare daggers at him and clap my flip-flops back to the kitchen to get the ketchup. I stop before entering when I hear my sister and mother talking in hushed tones. "Be patient with Sofia. She hasn't been the same since giving birth to Liam. She has convinced herself that you're the one who did all the things she did to you. Her baby daddy left long ago; you got married, but she still thinks your husband, John, is Ken and he has been following her around."

"Is she still taking her medication?"

"She insists she has never needed them."

I push the door open and enter the kitchen, and they go silent. "Hello, gossip girls," I murmur, picking up the ketchup before heading back to the living room.

Ivy follows with a tray of fruit salad. Immediately she places it on the table, Liam jumps and grabs a big piece of pineapple, and starts sucking the honey off of it. Apparently, etiquette is also not on the agenda of these private schools. My mom comes in, holding a plate of food for me and for herself, while Ivy shoots back into the kitchen to fix a plate for herself and Ken. I grab my plate and head upstairs to eat in my room.

I open my bedroom door to take my plate to the kitchen once they have left. I find my mom finishing up washing the dishes. "Liam was looking for you to say goodbye," she says. I ignore her, place my dirty plate in the sink, and disappear back to my room. I read a few pages of *The Sex Lives of African Women* before slipping into my nightdress and calling it a day.

I wake up early in the morning, ready to tarmac again. I have a good feeling about today. I glance at my bottle of antipsychotic medication. I haven't touched it in months, and I am not planning to. After taking a shower, changing my clothes, having breakfast, and brushing my teeth, I get fare and money for lunch from my mom and step out to try my luck again. As I walk toward the stage, I look around, tighten the grip on my handbag, and quicken my steps; I know—I know—I know he's out there somewhere, following me.

Dating Maureen

Paul walks quickly, glancing at his thin watch. He stops a lady in a white frock on the road. "Can you tell me where Kencom is? I'm late for a date with my wife." The lady looks at his uncombed hair and disheveled appearance, then hurries away without a word. "After that, I need to pick up my daughter from school," he mutters to himself, quickening his pace. He is panting now. The dark suit he wears is threadbare and dusty, has sweat stains under the arms, and his faded black leather shoes have holes near his big toe.

He stops a man in brown khakis, black vans, and a blue polo shirt. "Can you tell me where Kencom is? I'm late for a date with my wife." The man gives him a confused look. Paul checks his watch again. "The date was at 8:00 a.m. I'm an hour late." His flawless English is the only reason the man in the polo shirt pauses to listen. He raises an eyebrow, points to a large sign written 'KENCOM HOUSE' directly opposite Paul, and then hurries past the city clock, whose hour hand points to noon. Paul stops another lady. "Can you tell me where Kencom is? I'm late for a date with my wife."

Maureen watches him from her office window on the third floor of Kenya Commercial Bank. She steps away from the window, sits on her desk, and tries to focus on the monitor in front of her but can't. Restless, she stands again, straightens her gray skirt suit, and walks to the window. Her cream pumps make no sound on the soft blue office carpet. She sees Paul pacing up and down, mumbling to himself, stopping random passersby. When he tilts his head toward the sky, she quickly closes the blinds, walks back to her seat, and grips her mahogany desk.

Maureen is sweating, but it's not because of the midday sun. The beads of sweat on her forehead are the result of being overwhelmed by life—something that has been happening often lately. She rises from her mahogany desk and removes her coat, revealing damp patches under the arms of her cream blouse. She hangs the coat on the stand, locks the door to her office, and sits down again. Resting her head in her hands, she begins to sob. A single tear trickles down her cheek, landing on a white A4 paper, leaving a dark stain. Then, the tears come in a torrent, carving grooves through her foundation, and concealer.

She pulls a handkerchief from her desk drawer, and covers her face. The crying is muffled but the heaving makes her whole body convulse. After some time, the darkness ebbs, and her tears stop. She heads to the small bathroom in her office and emerges looking refreshed. She unlocks the door to her office, and opens the blinds on her window. Paul is still pacing, still mumbling, still stopping random people in his path. She glances at her watch, looks at him again, and remembers their first date.

Paul was starting out as an accountant at Housing Finance, while she was interning as a banker at Kenya Commercial Bank. They had chosen Java Kimathi, for their first date, as it was central to both of their workplaces.

She remembers trying out different outfits the previous night. First, she had picked out a green trouser suit then looked in the mirror and decided it was too uptight. She picked a blue dress with a plunging neckline, but then realized she wanted him to look at her during the date, not her chest. She had finally settled on black sandals, a cream blouse that revealed her arms, and a flowy red skirt whose hem stopped just before her knees, an outfit that said she was into banking, but she could also be into fun.

Sitting across from Paul, she'd realized she'd never gotten a chance to look at him properly. They had met briefly in the office while he was handling their accounting, but that hadn't given her enough time to take him in fully. Now, she was noticing details she hadn't noticed before—like how uncoordinated his outfit was. He wore a baggy yellow shirt, gray sweatpants, and black Toughees. His hair was bushy, and his watch was large and crass. If they started dating seriously, that outfit, the hair, and watch had to go. *There is no way I'm going to walk arm in arm with an ape*, she had thought.

The waiter brought their food. She remembers sending her plate back because it wasn't hot enough, and when it came back, steam rising from it, she had reached into her handbag and pulled out a bottle of homemade tomato sauce.

"It's healthier than the Heinz provided by the restaurant," she told Paul. Most men found her controlling, but Paul thought she was meticulous—and that was how their Java dates continued, and their fling began.

Maureen glances out the window again. Paul is no longer where her last gaze left him—he's walking towards the reception area of Kenya Commercial Bank.

"Can you tell me where Kencom is? I'm late for a date with my wife," he asks a guard. "After that, I need to pick up my daughter from school," he mumbles under his breath. He's a familiar face around here. The guards glance at each other knowingly. They have strict instructions on how to handle him—ignore him until he leaves. "Can you tell me where Kencom is? I'm late for a date with my wife." Paul is now at the foyer, talking to the receptionist.

Hope

MAUREEN OPENS THE door for her secretary, a slender girl dressed entirely in blue, who recently started working for her. The secretary asks how they should deal with the nuisance at the reception desk. Maureen asks her to give her a minute. The secretary walks out of the office, leaving the door open. Maureen sits at her desk and puts both of her palms on her face. She will have to redo her makeup again, she thinks with irritation.

When she removes her hands from her face, the first thing she sees is a passport-sized photo of her daughter, Hope. She had not wanted the memory to surface. It had come about by chance; earlier, when she had reached for a handkerchief in her drawer, the photo had fallen out. She had picked it up and put it on her desk without looking at it. Now, staring at it, she's forced to confront the full gravity of the situation.

She goes to the window, trying to push the memory away by focusing on the events that followed. It was a date at the tailor to get a few custom-made suits for Paul, and a trip to the watch store to finally get rid of the hideous thing on his wrist. His Toughees had disappeared unexpectedly, replaced by sleek Oxford leather shoes. In the early days of their relationship, Paul had welcomed these changes—even loved them—besides, he was having an effect on her too.

Maureen remembers enjoying frolicking, and being taken like a slutty college girl in mall washrooms, lifts, and changing rooms. She couldn't understand why she loved it so much. It was the one thing that wasn't proper about her. Paul often teased that she loved it because she was too uptight in college, forever buried in her big banking books. She tries to remember which mall, lift or store they conceived their daughter, Hope, but her head is heavy now—heavy with memory of that night that plunged her into darkness, and Paul into madness.

Their differences started to show when the baby came. They argued about how to raise her. Paul wanted the child to discover herself, while Maureen was more strict. The arguments didn't stop there—they spilled over into their relationship. Paul felt that, as the man, he should make the decisions, while Maureen believed that the one who earned the most should be in charge. She had thought it would inspire him, but instead, it put them on separate roads.

The sex fizzled. There were counseling sessions that didn't work, and weekly mandatory dates meant to rekindle their romance that fell flat. Some days, Maureen wished she could take back some of her words; other days, she wished for a stronger man. They began sleeping in separate rooms, and their union was reduced to mere appearances.

Paul started finding comfort in the bottle, sinking deeper into it, month after month, year after year to the point where he had been sent home on compulsory leave. By this time, Maureen had been promoted to Chief Banking Officer at Kenya Commercial Bank, while Paul remained an accountant at Housing Finance. Maureen started toying with the idea of sending Hope to a boarding school, reasoning that it was unhealthy for a child to be around a drunkard.

By then, Paul had reached the bottom of the bottle, and was coming to their Lavington home—whose mortgage Maureen had finally finished paying, in the wee hours of the night. After the guard had opened the gate for him, he would fumble with the lock, fall onto the couch, and wake up in the morning, have a shower, a change of clothes and leave.

They lived like roommates—less than roommates; more like enemies. They hadn't spoken to each other in over six months. Communication between them was done through their daughter.

"Go and tell Maureen..."

"Go and tell Paul..."

"Mom said to tell you…"

"Dad said to tell you…"

Paul lost his job and started disappearing for weeks at a time, and when he resurfaced, he was irritable. He would get up without warning, and start ironing Maureen's clothes, with the iron dial turned all the way up, burning holes into her favorite outfits. When he wasn't burning her clothes, he was in the kitchen, breaking her fine china.

One day, he was sitting on the couch, the alcohol draining from his head, when Hope approached and tapped him on the shoulder. "Dad, Mom said to tell you that if you continue like this, we're going to leave and never come back."

That fateful night, Hope was playing with her dolls in the living room, the TV turned to Disney Channel. Maureen was in the bedroom folding clothes. Paul came home early, and sober. He sat next to Hope and put a finger on her lips, "Shhh, we're going to Disney world," he whispered, picking her up and tiptoeing towards the door. He had barely touched the handle when Maureen showed up with a kitchen knife. One quick slash, and the floor was stained with red—only, the blood wasn't Paul's.

Paul went mad after that, and disappeared into the streets. When the police showed up, they assumed he had done it, and she didn't bother to correct them.

MAUREEN STEADIES HERSELF on her mahogany desk. Her knees are weak now. She holds onto the desk, but her strength and her grip are waning, and she collapses into a heap on the floor. She stares at the passport-sized photo of Hope, and a lone tear flows down her cheek, hitting the carpet with a soft plop. After that, a torrent follows. She's heaving now and convulsing, and crying out loudly and her secretary and everyone in the office is looking at her in disbelief, not knowing what to do because it's the first time they are seeing their boss out of grip.

She pulls herself up, still heaving, and takes the stairs instead of the lift—one step at a time, each heavier than the last. She finally reaches the reception area and she is face-to-face with the father of her daughter. Paul looks at her inquiringly, then opens his mouth to speak.

"Can you tell me where Kencom is? I'm late for a date with my wife."

Maureen takes his hand, and they walk out of the building, crossing City Hall Way towards Kimathi Street.

They sit in Java, sharing a meal. "I can't stay long, I'm late for a date with my wife. Do you know where Kencom is?" Paul asks, glancing at his thin watch—the same watch she had bought him for their *monthversary*. The watch that had stopped working years ago. "After that, I need to pick up my daughter from school," Paul continues, while Maureen scrolls through her phone.

She makes the first call to a mental hospital and the second to the police. *It's high time they knew the truth,* she thinks, and a smile almost touches her lips before the darkness engulfs her again.

Good Deeds

No bad deed goes unpunished. When I interact with someone, I open their file in my mind, recalling how they've treated me since our first encounter, and I reward or punish them accordingly. Everything is weighed on a scale; nothing escapes me. I am the judge, jury, and executioner. Some get away with a slap on the wrist, and others… well, others pay the ultimate price.

Even as I close the door to the basement before my date, I know my reward-and-punishment system will catch up with me someday. But today is not that day—and my nosy neighbor, Natalie, certainly won't be the one to unravel it. She came around, apparently to 'say hello' when really, it was just an excuse to gossip about our missing neighbors, Owen and Tracy. It doesn't help that they were my next-door neighbors. Oh, snooping Natalie. I've already opened her file, and perhaps I'll pay her a visit one of these days.

But enough about her—I have a hot date tonight. But first, I secure the basement door with three hardened padlocks and hide it behind a bookshelf. I look around my living room with a satisfied grin. The decor now says I'm a well-adjusted, upper-middle-class woman in her late 20s.

The black cat scratching the bookshelf, searching for a scent she can't quite find, is Kiwi. She indicates I'm crazy but not too crazy to keep more than one. The silver cross engraved with her name swings from her blue collar as she claws away at the wood.

A photo of me in a bikini with 'friends' in Diani hangs on the wall, suggesting I'm outgoing. Next to it, another photo of me in Paris, near the Eiffel Tower, and in London by the London Eye, says I'm well-traveled, able to afford more than the clothes on my back and the food in my belly. The sculpture of the smiling buddha on my TV stand hints that I'm a free spirit, superstitious, or crazier.

All in all, I'm decent enough to have scored a date with an eligible Nairobi bachelor. God knows those are hard to come by nowadays. I take one last look in my full-length mirror. The small butterfly tattoo on my ankle says I'm hip without being ratchet, and the little white dress with a plunging neckline I'm wearing suggests he might get lucky tonight if he plays his cards right. *Will he play his cards right, or will he fumble the bag? And if he does, will he get away with a slap on the wrist, or will he pay the ultimate price?* I wonder, slipping into my red bottoms and heading out.

Wine and Di(e)ne

God is always making men; some are tall, others short. Some hate women, and others love them too much. Some shower three times a day, while others don't believe in soap. Some are cruel, and others are cowards. But every once in a while, you come across a proper man who makes you rethink your singlehood, and I'm lucky enough to be seated across from one.

Moses is in his late 30s, wearing a black three-piece suit. His face is covered with a full beard, and there is a twinkle in his eye as he smiles at me. We've been talking for an hour, yet it feels as though I've known him for a lifetime. He's a writer, a master of ceremonies, and a marathon runner. He's one of those men who go around the world succeeding at everything they do—you could almost resent him. He reveals his perfect pair of teeth again and his devilish smile cuts me open like a dagger. *Moses, oh Moses, take me to the promised land.*

"Your keyholder is unique." He sets his empty wine glass down, picks up my keys from the table, and starts fiddling with the cat-shaped design. *A man who pays attention to detail.* I think and smile, sipping the last dregs of my sweet red.

He picks a key. "What does this one open?" he asks, looking at me with a playful grin. I smile nervously. "Let me guess—it's the key to your heart," he adds.

I giggle. "It's one of those things that if I told you, I'd have to kill you."

"I'm already dead from your killer looks," he flatters.

"Let's get out of here," I say, grabbing the keys from his hand.

"Do you have a location in mind?"

"My place."

I told you, it's not every day you meet a proper man in Nairobi, but when you do, you grab the bull by the horns. And this one—this Moses—I'm going to let him part my legs like the Red Sea.

He parks his BMW X5 in my townhouse driveway in Spring Valley, gets out, and opens the passenger door for me. I'm hot and bothered, and I can't quite open the door to my house. "Let me," he says from behind, taking the keys from my hands. I get even more bothered as his warm palms glide over the back of my hands.

Kiwi has been busy looking for the scent she can't quite find when we enter the house. In her search, she's knocked a couple of books off the shelf, revealing the basement door. But Moses' eyes are too fixed on my cleavage to notice. When he raises them, I distract him further by plunging my tongue deep into his mouth—I think I touch his tonsils.

My white dress and his three-piece-suit soon form a puddle on the floor. He is in my burning bush, taking me to the promised land again and again and again. I raise my head to gasp for air. I didn't imagine you could go to the promised land that many times. *I will keep this one*, I think, as he removes the rubber from his now flaccid penis, and I go to freshen up, having forgotten all about my bookshelf.

"Three padlocks. What are you hiding in there?" I come back from the bathroom to find him inspecting the door behind the bookshelf.

"Don't!" I hear myself bark, but he has my keys and is unlocking the third padlock. The next thing I know, Moses is lying still on the floor, the smiling buddha sculpture shattered beside his head.

Church Woman

"Forgive me, father, for I have sinned. It has been 28 days since my last confession. I have harbored feelings of jealousy, lust, hate, and wrath." I wipe the film of tears from my eyes and begin my confession to the priest but first, some preamble.

No bad deed should go unpunished. This is true. But what happens when you come across someone like Moses? Someone who's done you no harm, yet somehow, you end up harming them? What's your retribution then—a slap on the wrist or the ultimate price?

After taking care of Moses and his personal effects, I find myself at the Holy Family Basilica, garbed in a long black frock, chapel veil, and sandals. Nosy, nosy Moses—who snoops around someone's house on the first day? I try to convince myself that he had it coming as I walk through the gates of the church. *Come to me all ye who are weary and burdened and I will give you rest.* I glance at the noticeboard as I enter the confessional room.

"Forgive me, Father, for I have sinned…" I continue between sobs and short, tight hiccups. "I've wished ill on my neighbors. I've dressed provocatively, fornicated, and recently, I put down a bird that had done me no harm. I detest all my sins and firmly resolve, with the help of your grace, to sin no more."

"He deserves my tears," I murmur, wiping the last film of water from my eyes. "Huuhh," I exhale a sigh like air from a deflated balloon. *There is a catharsis to confessing,* I think as I leave the church. Sure, I embellished some things and told half-truths, but the knot in my stomach has loosened—I feel lighter.

I pass by Carrefour to pick up cleaning supplies and spend the better part of my afternoon on my knees, scrubbing the red smudge from my floor as Kiwi scratches at the bookshelf. I'm startled from my kneeling position by the ring of my doorbell.

"Hello, are you Edna?" A rugged, outdoorsy-looking man asks after I open the door and I nod. "Might you have seen my brother?" He holds up a picture of Moses, leaning against his BMW. He must have traced him here through traffic cameras. My mind works over time trying to figure out how he's standing at my door. "Your neighbor Natalie, was kind enough to mention she saw what looked like his BMW in your driveway." I smile nervously. *Natalie, oh snooping Natalie. Forgive me, Father, for I am about to sin again.*

Friends Without Benefits

"THIS ISN'T A good time," I say flatly, beginning to close the door on the stranger holding Moses's picture.

"Reach me on this line if anything comes up," he says politely, handing me a card.

I close the door, toss the card labeled 'Jim's Pub' into the bin, and pace across my living room. "Fuck!" I bark, making Kiwi jump off the bookshelf, startled. "Did Natalie see me switching the plates on Moses's BMW before I drove it upcountry and sank it underneath the waves of Lake Naivasha?" I mumble, opening Natalie's folder in my mind and recalling how we first met.

I had just broken up with my then-boyfriend, God rest his soul—who also happened to be my neighbor. Our passion burned hot, and we agreed to stay friends with benefits, as we worked out the grubby details of moving on.

His name was Owen, and it was love at first sight. Hellos turned to introductions, and introductions into dreams of being together. Sweet agony, isn't it? Wanting someone, knowing they want you back, and feeling that it's just a matter of time before the inevitable happens.

The inevitable happened, and we quickly became an item, and broke up just as quickly. You could believe the lie that I was too jealous, or the truth that he had no boundaries.

All the same, there I was, knocking on his door, claiming I'd forgotten my earrings at his place. It was about time I started enjoying these benefits, wouldn't you agree? Instead, he opened the door in a bathrobe, Natalie hiding her nakedness behind him. "This is not a good time," he said, shutting the door in my face.

It wasn't a good day either because that was the same day he disappeared—and the day I opened Natalie's 'file' in my mind. She came by later to apologize. I told her that Owen and I had broken up and that she shouldn't lose sleep over it. After that, she decided we were friends.

I take a shower and change into a cream sweater and blue jeans. I pace the length of the living room one more time before heading to the kitchen. Turning on the burner, I fill a *sufuria* with water. As it starts to boil, I pick up my phone and dial Natalie.

"Hi, Nat. I've got some tea about Owen…is this a good time?"

"It's perfect," she chirps, and I can hear her rushing for the door. I tap the red receiver and smile to myself, feeling a nervous thrill.

Nata(lie)

GOD IS ALWAYS making women. Some are loving, others caring, some sweet, others brave, but every once in a while, you meet a woman and can't quite decide what she contributes to society. That woman is now knocking on my door, as if it's her right to be let in.

"It's cold and scary dark out here. Open up!" Natalie complains.

I open the door to the sound of chewing gum and the smell of vanilla-scented smoke. "Want a puff?" she asks, extending a vape pen.

"Maybe later," I say.

"Come on, live a little." She presses the pen into my hand.

I glance at her after closing the door. Her hair is dyed pink, and she's wearing a pink off-shoulder top, miniskirt, and green platform heels to match her green choker and green eyeshadow. She looks like the kind of girl who's constantly getting into tricky situations thanks to peer pressure.

"Would you like something to drink?" I ask, though what I really want to ask is if she's on midterm break.

"I will take a gin or anything strong," she says, plopping herself onto the sofa that Kiwi had been lying on. Kiwi jumps and scurries under the table. "Have you heard the latest lingo in town?" she asks, oblivious to displacing my pet while blowing a large bubble with her gum. I shake my head as it explodes on her face.

"It's called *shembeteng*," she explains. I raise a brow. "*Wabambataba wanalombotov wamambatama wa mchembetele.*" I ignore her and head to the kitchen. "It loosely translates to, *wababa wanapenda wamama wa mchele*," she shouts, mid-chew.

A minute with Natalie, and I already have a headache. *Luckily, it'll be the last minute I ever spend with her,* I think and smile while placing her nasty vape pen on the countertop. I turn off the burner, make myself a cup of hot chocolate and pour Gin into a glass and mix it with, ahm, what did she call it? Yes, *mchele*—enough to put an elephant to sleep—and take it to her.

"What's the tea on Owen?" she whispers as I place her drink on the table and take a seat. She blows another bubble, and when it pops, I feel flecks of gum on my lip and I want to strangle her with her choker.

"You need to be tipsy for this," I say, taking a sip from my hot chocolate. She reaches for her glass, but her hand knocks it over. "I'm so clumsy," she giggles, standing up to clean the mess she's created. As she does, I catch a glimpse of what looks like a pistol tucked into the waistband of her skirt. *God is always making women,* I think. Some are loving, others sweet, and some are not who they pretend to be.

Bestie

THE OTHER MISSING neighbor was called Tracy. She thought she was clever—oh, this one hurt the most. She'd made me believe she was my best friend, only to realize she kept me around because I made her feel better about herself. How could that be, you wonder?

Oh, I'm such a lonely Tracy.

But at least I'm not as lonely as Edna.

I could be a fashionable Tracy.

But at least I'm not as old-fashioned as Edna.

I could be a slimmer Tracy.

But at least I'm not as out of shape as Edna.

You get the picture, don't you? Did I get rid of her because of this? No, I'm not that petty, though I'll admit, her attitude sparked the determination I needed to make changes, not out of spite, but because I could. You see, money was never a problem. Like Portia from *Merchant of Venice*, you could say I'm richly left. I won't bore you with the sordid details of what happened to my husband. I'm pretty sure you can guess what went down. *His file was opened and the ultimate price was paid.* See, you catch on quick.

Back to Tracy. As I said, I'm not petty, not where someone's life could be on the line, but I did go about trying to prove her wrong. I hit the gym and trimmed down to a size eight, got myself a skincare routine, and revamped my wardrobe. Trips to Mombasa, London, and Paris followed, and soon enough, men and women alike were stumbling over themselves to invite me to their parties, and guess who wasn't happy? Moses? No, Tracy.

She started spreading rumors around the neighborhood that I was a witch. My black cat, Kiwi, and husband's mysterious disappearance didn't help. I could handle all that, but then she began telling people my husband was locked in my basement. Now, that was a step too far. If that kind of rumor gained traction, the police could start snooping around. The last thing I wanted was them to show up at my doorstep with a search warrant and so I had to do something about it.

I invited her over and told her I wanted to make amends. *I'd even show her the basement because I am an open book with nothing to hide.* That day, I dressed down—on makeup, and wore a drab brown dera and we were right back to Tracy feeling better about herself. God knows I could have kept up that charade forever, but then she said she was ready to see what was in my basement.

One by one, I unlocked the three padlocks, swung open the door and flicked on the lights. "After you," I said. She took a step forward and I pushed her down the flight of stairs. The only part of her that screamed was her skull, cracking open from the impact of her fall, being broken by a brick wall.

Hidden in the Basement

Natalie is flashing her police badge and gun in my face. Come to think of it, she moved into the neighborhood after Tracy disappeared. Talk about deep cover. Her face has shifted, transforming from that of a laid-back teen to a hardened officer who means business, and I find myself lifting my hands in the air without being told.

"Edna, I'm going to have to insist to see what's behind your bookshelf," she barks, her singsong voice replaced by a steely tone.

"There's nothing to see there, Nat—just old, rust-covered equipment and a lot of dust," I say, trying to keep my tone casual, while my mind works overtime, thinking of how to get myself out of this fix, but judging from the defiant look on Natalie's face, it looks like my goose is cooked. "I will need the key to open the padlocks," I add, glancing at the hook where they hang.

She nods, eyes trained on me, and I pick up the keys. She follows closely, her gun aimed at my back. *I have my hands back. I might still have a chance to get myself out of this,* I think as I push the bookshelf aside and open the padlocks, one after the other. When I swing the door open and switch on the lights, I step back. "After you."

"It's your basement," she says. "You lead, I follow." Her eyes narrow. "Hands where I can see them." she adds and I am back to being handless.

"You won't find anything down here, Nat, except for souvenirs, broken appliances, and old clothes," I emphasize as we pass a box full of knick-knacks that she doesn't give a second glance. She could have found a few things that would have surprised her. That's the thing about people, they refuse to see what's right under their noses.

"Guess souvenirs smell like death these days?" she sneers as Kiwi runs ahead of us, leading the way. I suppose, in a way, she is more curious than all of us because what is ahead could mean a meal for her.

We reach the source of the stench. "Open the damn freezer," Natalie commands, her grip tightening on the gun. I hesitate, then swing the lid of the rectangular chest freezer open. The smell hits both of us like a wave and we cover our noses and step back.

Still covering her nose, Natalie approaches the freezer again and starts rifling through packets of bacon, sausages, goat, beef, and pork chops that I keep in it because they can't fit in my kitchen fridge—with a disappointed look on her face. *Its fuse must have blown*, I think, grabbing Kiwi from inside the freezer and carrying her on my bosom.

"See, Nat," I say, straightening. "I told you there's nothing to see down here."

She tucks her gun back into her waistband, looking a little embarrassed. "You should clean that out and call an electrician."

"And you should tell people the truth about who you really are," I say cheerfully, guiding her to the door. With that, I know our tea-time chats about Owen—and the rumors about my basement—have come to an end. I toss her vape pen into the bin with a smirk. "Two birds, one stone."

Out of the Closet

Bodies can be buried; flesh and bones dissolve in acid. So you shouldn't be asking where the bodies went. But one, in particular, I couldn't bring myself to get rid of. I mean, it's not every day you find an eligible Nairobi bachelor who's good to you, and good for you.

I walk the length of my sitting room, climb the stairs and reach what was once my closet, but now Moses's residence. He is secured in chains and I drug his drinks to make sure he doesn't get ideas. You might be saying that is no way for a man to live but the alternative is worse, isn't it?

He is withering more with each day. I suppose the drugs have taken their toll. Still, I remember when he used to be in high spirits. Times when I would give him a sponge bath, a change of clothes, and a hearty meal. He is a man after all and he still gets sexual urges like every other hot-blooded male, and maybe I did or didn't let him part my legs like the red sea.

But the fun and games are gone. Now he mostly exists in a vegetative state, drooling on his shirt, pissing and shitting on himself and soiling my carpet, and I'm always the one doing the hard work of cleaning after him.

I find him in that same state today. The state that is making me resent him. I change his diapers and leave him in the company of Kiwi. He has taken a liking to her even though, at first, he wanted nothing to do with the pet. "Demon!" he would bark at the poor thing. That is of course before his speech slurred and the words completely left his voice box.

I throw his used diapers in the dustbin and wonder if perhaps it's time for Moses to join Owen, Tracy, and all of them. I mean, Moses removed the Israelites from Egypt but he did not see Canaan. It's Biblical. "Tonight," I say to myself and make a mental note to go for Confession at the Holy Family Basilica the next day.

Kiwi

KIWI IS PLAYING with the hem of Moses's shirt as the silver cross on his collar swings back and forth. She is excitable like every cat is when someone shows it a little attention. She begins to lick the drool from his chin, and Moses picks her up, and fiddles with her collar before shooing her away with unwarranted hostility. With a startled meow, Kiwi darts from the bedroom, down the stairs, and into the sitting room where she finds Edna.

"I'm off to buy some supplies at Carrefour. I'll be back in an hour." Kiwi hears the voice of Edna that she is already used to by now. Edna opens the door and as she does, Kiwi dashes past her and out into the next-door neighbor's yard, just as an Uber pulls up.

"Come back here, Kiwi. What did we say about going into other people's houses?" Kiwi hears Edna's voice raise but she is busy squatting and shitting on the grass. The engine of the car hums and she watches the grey-shaped box with black round things disappear into the horizon.

"Meow," she sings, now sunbathing on the grass, opposite her excrement while licking her charcoal-black fur. She is distracted again and is now jumping from one stone to the other and she is soon on the roof of the house. She finds a stray cat there. "Meow," she screams aggressively to mark her territory.

When that fails, her claws come out. Both cats roll around on the roof, making angry noises. After some time, Kiwi stands and runs away. She will have a bowl of milk and a hot meal waiting for her at home, she remembers. She doesn't need to die on the roof to some stray cat in the name of a turf war.

The sun dips lower in the sky. Kiwi finds herself on the opposite side of the road, leaping over the flower pot of another yard and climbing through a slightly cracked window into a stranger's bedroom. "Meow," she purrs softly to the unfamiliar surroundings. Then she sees a familiar person dressed in pink applying green eye shadow on her face and sits on the bed.

"What are you doing here?" Natalie asks Kiwi as if she can understand the words while picking her up. "Who hurt you?" she murmurs concerned, looking at the gaping wound next to the cat's blue collar, and as she does she sees a folded white piece of paper tucked next to the silver cross that is almost falling off. "What is this?" she asks, unfolding it and reading aloud. "I'm in her bedroom closet. Help!"

With urgency, Natalie stands, cradling Kiwi in one arm while reaching for her pistol with the other. She slips it into her waistband, wears flip-flops, and storms out of her house, crossing the road with purpose.

"Thank you for bringing her back. What did we say about going into other people's houses?" Kiwi hears the familiar voice and warmth of her owner, Edna and meows.

"There is something else; I will need to see your bedroom," Natalie says. Kiwi can feel herself slipping from Edna's hands and like all cats, she lands on her feet and sees Edna running. She doesn't run far before Natalie tackles her to the ground and handcuffs her. Not long after that, their doorstep is filled with sirens. Edna disappears in the backseat of a police car and Moses is brought out of the house on a stretcher before he disappears inside an ambulance.

Edna

DURING THE COURT proceedings I learned that Natalie had adopted Kiwi and moved, probably to another undercover mission. Moses stayed with his brother, Jim as he recuperated. He bounced back and he was back to work within a week. I suppose besides being a writer, a master of ceremonies, and marathoner, he was also an actor.

As for me, they found the souvenirs and DNA traces from all my victims and so I'm being guarded 24/7 like some rabid dog. Can you believe it? Harmless little old me? They have chained my wrists and ankles and I can barely get into the armored van as they transfer me from my holding cell in Spring Valley Police Station to Langata Women's Prison.

I barely wonder who my cellmates will be; I'm immediately thrust into solitary confinement upon arrival. It is a small box with a high ceiling and very little light filtering through tiny crevices at the top. So it's mostly dark in here.

There is a bed in one corner with a King James Bible on top of it. *It will come in handy if I ever need to confess*, I think, and grin. In the other corner is a stainless steel toilet with tissue paper, and that's just about it.

Twice a day, Constable Josephine brings me food through a hole in the door, and twice every week, she brings me toilet paper and allows me to have a shower and a change of clothes. I have been observing Josephine for a while now. She could be a Tracy or even a Natalie.

Today, she didn't talk to me much besides bark commands.

My tea had sugar last week, but this week it did not.

The food was saltier this month than it was last month.

The blue striped uniform she brought this year had stains on it, while last year's did not.

I open her 'file' in my mind and weigh everything she has done to me on a scale. *Should she get a slap on the wrist or should she pay the ultimate price?* I wonder.

Eight Years Of Toxic Love

This is a true story. It contains violence in the form of physical and sexual abuse. If you find these topics triggering, please skip it. The person has chosen to remain anonymous, after you read her story, you will understand why. As she narrated the events, I couldn't shake the taste of pain from my mouth, and at times, it felt as if a knife was being dragged though my heart. I tip my hat to her for keeping her composure throughout the three hours or so we spoke. I hope this story serves as a teacher and a mirror to all of us.

I ignored the first red flag. My boyfriend loved to party, while I preferred the indoors. Nightclubs are loud and cold by nature, and I longed for the softness and warmth of my bed. Once, when we were out, I protested, saying I wanted to go home and sleep. He grabbed me and shook me. "Stop embarrassing me in front of my friends," he barked. "Just try and have a good time, eh?" He softened only after his friends calmed him down. From that night on, I never protested again, fearing I might trigger his anger. Little did I know, this was only the beginning of a descent into a rabbit hole of terror and pain that would leave me scarred physically and emotionally.

2012

I MET MY boyfriend in 2012 during my first year at The University of Nairobi. A naive 19-year-old girl from Kisii, feeling the thrill of the city's freedom for the first time. I was set to pursue Anthropology, but my heart gravitated towards Law. After speaking to my dad, I registered for Law on a parallel program while living in a private hostel off-campus. It was around this time that a friend introduced me to my boyfriend—a 24-year-old hunk in his third year, studying Design. He was tall, dark, handsome and charming, and I took to him immediately. To this day, I tell people what he's capable of and they stare, unbelieving. "Him? But he's such a charming guy."

You see, I didn't know how to cook. When I visited him at his third-floor hostel in campus, he would do most of the cooking. Most of the time, he made *ugali*, *sukuma*, and scrambled eggs in that tiny space that felt like a shoebox. But none of that mattered; we were in love. After eating, we'd crank up the music to drown the moaning and groaning sounds from our lovemaking. Our fling continued for about three months before we decided to make things official. I found myself spending more time at his place, and that's when his true colors began to show.

One night, he decided to leave me behind when he went partying. When he returned in the dead of night, he asked why I hadn't cooked. I told him he should have said something because I had already gotten some fries for myself. Besides, he knew I didn't know how to cook. He locked the door, pocketed the key, and turned up the music. "Today you'll understand who the man of this house is," he roared. What followed was a beating like I'd never seen before. He rained blows on me with both his fists and his feet. I'm small—40 kilograms and 5'3"—and he's double my size, at 80 kilograms, 6'. I felt like a bag of feathers being bounced off the walls.

"I want to leave," I screamed, my voice drowned out by the blaring music.

"You want to leave, eh?" He opened the window. "Then go ahead and leave." I felt so deperate that I climbed onto the window, ready to take my chances with gravity than with him. But before I could, he snapped back to his senses.

"Come down. You want people to say I killed you? If you want to leave, all you have to do is give me a blowjob, and I'll give you the key, and you can go." He'd just beaten me to a pulp, and yet his manhood was as hard as stone. Terrified of another beating, I got on my knees, fumbled with his belt, and took him in my mouth. After that, he had his way with me. It wasn't until five years later that I realized it was rape—because there had been no consent. Afterward, he lay beside me, crying as he held me close. "I'm sorry. It'll never happen again," he whispered between hiccups. Little did I know this was just a preview of what was to come.

2013

AT THE START of 2013, I found out I was pregnant. When I told him, he flew into a rage. "I'm still young. I want to enjoy myself. Are you trying to trap me?" he spat. At this time, he was also seeing three other women. I'd seen the suggestive texts on his phone:

The other night was great.

Babe, when can I see you again?

I miss you.

The conversations all revolved around sex, and when I confronted him, he didn't even deny it. "I'm a man. I need to sow my seed. I need to do these things before we get married. And anyway, I come home to you, not to any of those girls," he said without remorse. Oddly, it never crossed my mind to leave him, not even when he told me to get rid of the baby.

There's a pill called Cytotec, Misoprostol. You swallow two, and insert two in your vagina and as long as you're under three months pregnant, the abortion is a success. The pills cost around 2,000 Kenya shillings. My boyfriend didn't have the money and he told me to make up a story to get it from my parents.

I was with my friend when I took the pills. The pain was excruciating, lasting a full hour. It felt as if someone was dragging a knife through my insides. "You should leave him now," my friend cried, but her words fell on deaf ears. Later, my boyfriend came by, gave me a half-hearted sideways hug, and even had me give him 200 shillings for fare back to town.

Around that time I had the abortion, his anger flared again. He had asked me to cook *ugali*, but I had done a terrible job. This time, I wasn't willing to take a beating. I slipped out the door, ran, and hid in the hostel bathrooms. I could hear him knocking on doors, asking other students if they had seen me. When he finally found me, his anger had ebbed, and he told me he'd teach me to cook and clean. "*Hutakuwa unanipikia ugali mbichi. Lazima ujue kupika na kufanya kazi.*" He wanted his meals hot, and his clothes and duvets cleaned weekly. So there I was, both maid and plaything, and in my mind, all of it was love.

After that, things improved. Most of 2013 was good. He started this tradition of throwing birthday parties for me, gathering his friends to suprise me and always gifting me dresses. He never knew how much I disliked wearing them, so I'd smile and pretend to love it.

He never wanted to use protection. "Why would I? You are my woman?" he'd say. "*Si* it's only me you're fucking? Why are you even suggesting that we use protection?" He also didn't want me to take contraceptives, arguing they'd make me gain weight. I didn't dare take them, though in hindsight, he'd probably never have known.

Toward the end of 2013, right before he finished school, I got pregnant again. We were on a long holiday, and I was in my second year of Law School and first year of my newly added second major in Political Science and Philosophy. When I told him, he was still not ready. "I'm just getting out of campus," he said. "We're doing the same thing as before." This time, he bought the pills, was there for the abortion, and finally agreed to contraceptives. "We're having too many scares," he admitted.

Just before he graduated, he told me about a friend moving out of the staff quarters nearby. He suggested I move in—the rent was 6,000 Kenya shillings a month, the same as my private hostel, but with more privacy and space. He even suggested I move in with a friend to share the cost. But he must have convinced her otherwise; after we'd planned everything, and my dad had already sent the rent, she bailed.

2014

I MOVED INTO the SQ in March of 2014, just me, my laptop, a mattress, and an electric cooker. My boyfriend started visiting casually, spending the night now and then. Slowly, he began bringing his belongings, and before long, he'd moved in.

At the time, he was searching for a job, though he never actually found one. "I'm tired of looking for employment. I'll just do my own thing," he said one day, frustrated. He started his own design company, and it's been successful so far.

In December of 2014, he landed a big project in his hometown, Nakuru, thanks to a friend who set him up with the gig. I was deep in my exams and couldn't go with him, though I wanted to—we were so used to spending our evenings together. While he was away, he'd call often. "I miss you so much. Once your exams are done, come visit me," he'd say.

After exams, I went back home to Kisii. I couldn't shake off my restlessness, so I eventually worked up the courage to ask my dad if I could visit him. "Dad, I have a boyfriend in Nakuru, and I want to go and see him," I said, full of excitement and the bold confidence of youth. My dad, always easy-going, agreed. He even gave me fare for around trip, on the condition that I'd stay just one night and keep in touch while I was there.

My mom protested, but my dad cut her short.

"Let her make her own decisions. It's the only way she'll grow," he said firmly.

2015

AT THE END of 2014, I got pregnant again. Before my boyfriend went to Nakuru, we had another discussion about contraceptives. He told me that his married cousin had warned him against using them, claiming they could affect my fertility in the future when I wanted to have a baby. So, I stopped taking them.

Sometimes, I feel as if I wouldn't have gotten pregnant if my dad hadn't allowed me to go to Nakuru.

His Nakuru gig ended. I came back from Kisii and we were back together in Nairobi. I was juggling two degrees, and I wasn't ready for a baby. But this time, my boyfriend was. "I don't think this is the best time to have a child," I told him. "How are we supposed to raise a baby when we're sleeping on a mattress on the floor, and I'm struggling with school?"

He flew into a rage.

"How dare you tell me you're not ready when I'm working? How can you be so selfish? We'll have this baby and figure out your school later.

I told him that he would have to break the news to my parents, because honestly, I was embarrassed. How would I explain to them that I went to school for a degree and ended up with a baby? "No. You will tell them because they don't know me yet. But I'll help you with school," he insisted. "It doesn't make sense to defer your studies because of a baby."

I went home to break the news when I was three months pregnant. My dad, a retired doctor, and my mom, a retired nurse, knew right away when I arrived. They were just waiting for me to say it. On the last day before returning to Nairobi, I finally sat them down and told them. "I knew you were pregnant the moment you walked in," my mom admitted. "We're grateful you didn't think of having an abortion," they both added.

They assured me of their support and said it was okay if I wanted to defer school. When they asked about my boyfriend, I painted him as the nicest guy in the world. "He just graduated in December and he is working hard to provide for us," I told them, without as much as a hint of the darker side of his personality.

2015 was not a good year for me. Everything felt overwhelming, and I was exhausted most of the time. On top of a pregnancy and two degrees, I was living with a demanding boyfriend who wouldn't let anyone else handle his laundry or make his food. We didn't have running water, and I was usually the one fetching it from outside. Sometimes, the neighbors would take pity and help me carry it.

While it was a difficult year for me, it was a good one for my boyfriend. He was excited that we were having a boy and became more focused on work. Money started coming in, and he bought a bed, a carpet, a sofa, and a TV—all around my birthday in July, after throwing me his signature surprise party, complete with a dress. Obama was also visiting Kenya that month. "*Wacha tununue* TV *ndiyo hata sisi tuone* Obama," he said. He even got a GoTV decoder. It finally felt like we were moving up in life.

He started getting broke again at the end of 2015, when I was around seven months pregnant. We started having shouting matches. My hormones were flaring, and his behavior didn't help. He would come home around three in the morning, drunk, demanding freshly prepared food, and if his clothes weren't spotless, he'd get pissed.

"I work all day. When I get back, I want peace and quiet," he'd say. "Don't make me ask for things you should already know."

It became routine—he'd come home late, demand food, and clean clothes and we'd argue. "Just eat wherever you are," I'd snap. "I spend all day in school, I come home tired and I'm pregnant. You should be cooking and cleaning for me." My days involved commuting between my Political Science and Philosophy classes at the main campus, then rushing to Law School before finally getting home around 9:30 p.m.

"No, it's your wifely duty to take care of me," he'd bark.

One Saturday night, he came home drunk, around 10:30 p.m., earlier than usual. As soon as he walked in, he began berating me. At this point, my hormones were already frayed, so I talked back. What set him off was when I said I would leave and go back to my parents. He grabbed a *mwiko* and beat me until it broke. Then he grabbed a knife.

"You're stressing me out too much. *Si* you want to kill me? Take this knife and kill me because I can't come to my own house and just relax. Take the knife and kill me. If you don't, I will kill you. You and my son will die tonight."

I was terrified, for both myself and the baby. I tried to calm him. "Think about our son. Think about how happy you'll be when he's born." He started raining blows on me and I crouched against the wall to protect my belly.

"If you won't take this knife and kill me, I'm going to kill you."

Then, out of nowhere, he stopped. It was as if something clicked in him, a realization that he shouldn't be hitting the mother of his child. He began crying. "I'm sorry. I didn't mean for it to get this far." We were both crying. I thought I would leave him then, but then I wondered what I'd be leaving for—to go back to the village to be laughed at? So I forgave him. In my head, I thought things would improve after the baby was born.

They didn't. They got worse.

I gave birth in October 2015. We were broke. Without my dad's help, we'd have had nothing. After giving birth, I realized I didn't have the friends I thought I had. No one came to check up on me. No one thought, *"Let's get together and visit her with diapers."* I tore up bedsheets to use during the day and saved the one 30 shillings diaper we could afford each day for nighttime. It wasn't enough because newborns poop all the time.

My boyfriend didn't help at all with the baby. When I was feeding or changing him, he'd either be out drinking or fast asleep, claiming it was my "womanly duty". On top of it, he still wanted sex. One night, he came home drunk, and started demanding for it.

"The doctor said we shouldn't have sex until after three months because I need to heal," I tried to explain, but he wouldn't hear it.

"I don't care what the doctor said, you're my wife. I have the right to have sex when I want," he insisted. When I resisted, he got physical, and I gave in. I started bleeding heavily, and he sobered up, asking if I was on my period.

I started to check out of school. I'd attend class, but nothing registered. Milk would leak through my blouse during lectures, and I'd rush back home afterward. I became so detached that a lecturer eventually asked, "Are you sure you're ready for exams?"

"Yes, I am," I replied defiantly, and he went on to fail me.

Looking back, I should have taken a year off. But my boyfriend kept pushing.

"Show your parents you can do this. Don't make it look like you can't handle things now that you have a child."

I had exams in November, right after the baby was born. We did not have a nanny. We did not even have money to buy a breast pump so the baby would only have milk whenever I was around. When I rushed to school for exams, my boyfriend would stay with the baby. When he cried, he would sanitize his hands and let the baby suck his thumb. This went on for about a week, then he put in around 200 shillings and I chipped in 300 shillings from what my dad sent me, and we bought a bottle.

I wasn't allowed to tell my parents we were struggling. My boyfriend would get pissed whenever my dad sent me money. "Are you trying to show your parents that I can't take care of you and the baby?"

I was done with exams and December was here, and we were getting ready to visit my parents for Christmas. "There's no way my son will travel in a *matatu*," my boyfriend insisted, hiring a car for 3,000 Kenya shillings even though he only had 4,000 shillings. His mom and dad are separated. There was a back and forth between them about who would take him to see my parents. They eventually declined and his cousin, who ended up fueling the hired car, came instead.

When we got to Kisii town, we went to a nearby supermarket with our remaining 1,000 shillings to get my folks something. I remember the exact amount we spent: 573 Kenya shillings after buying two kilograms of sugar, one bar of soap and the big Ketepa tea leaves. When we got home, my mom had told the whole village that her in-laws were coming and they had cooked up a storm. The women were there waiting and it was just me, the baby, him and his cousin. My mom was so sad about it. "*Mnaniaibisha aje hivyo?*" she whispered to me later.

My boyfriend was not embarrassed at all. The funny thing is, he got along with my parents. They said they liked him. He's a charmer, conversations come so easily for him. If you met him before I told you anything about him, you wouldn't believe me. He charmed the socks off their feet.

When we left Kisii, my folks thought they had a model son-in-law and I had the greatest husband in the world.

2016

I CAME BACK to Nairobi in January of 2016 after staying with my parents for two weeks, and it was back to the same old struggle. My boyfriend was still doing design gigs, but they were few and far between. I had no money, barely any food, while he was out partying every other night. When he came home, he either wanted food, despite having left no money, or sex—something I didn't have the energy or appetite for anymore.

My sex drive had completely disappeared. When I refused him, he would get furious. "Do you want me to start sleeping around?" he'd threaten. Scared, I'd give in, lying there like a log while he did as he pleased.

He'd complain, "Why are you so dry? Don't I excite you anymore? Or is someone else out there keeping you busy?"

I began to hate sex. My past started haunting me—the abortions, his abuse, being constantly broke, struggling with school and a baby—they all started weighing on me, and I sank into depression.

I didn't graduate in 2016 as planned. I missed all my Political Science exams and only managed to do a handful of Law School ones. I'd stand outside the exam room, thinking, *What's the point of doing these exams, if I'm going to fail?*

Most times I would just go back home. When my boy-friend asked how the exam went, I'd lie and say it was fine. Partly out of guilt, partly to avoid his anger. "See? We can do this. There was no need for you to defer school," he'd say, proud, though I couldn't tell if he was happy for me or just happy I was doing what he wanted.

Just before my birthday in July, we got a nanny. It was my mom's idea. "How are you managing without help?" she asked, and she sent us someone from the village. We were still struggling, but my boyfriend managed to pay her most of the time, and when he couldn't, I'd secretly ask my parents to help.

For my birthday, my friend called, and told me she was in town, and she wanted to buy me pizza. When we got back to my place, it turned out to be another of my boyfriend's "surprise" birthday parties. All my friends, and his friends were there. The baby was crawling around eating cake, and he'd bought me another dress.

Things got slightly better after that. In August, just before my son turned one, I got a job on Instagram that paid me 10,000 Kenya shillings, monthly. Fashion had always been my thing, and a woman opening a shop at the Mirage in Westlands hired me, letting me work and attend school. That money covered rent, the nanny, diapers, and groceries. "Looks like you're becoming responsible. See? Giving you a baby was a good thing," my boyfriend said when I first brought home the bacon. But by then, I was already thinking about leaving him.

He hadn't changed. He still partied whenever he had any money. One night, he came home completely drunk, needing his friend to support him. He stumbled in, vomited all over the carpet, and passed out on his own fluids. I grabbed a mop, put it under his head, and left him there. The next morning, he woke up, furious. "Why did you leave me on the floor? Are you trying to embarrass me in front of the nanny?" he yelled. And I just stood there, wondering how a 40 kilogram woman was supposed to move an 80 kilogram man.

December knocked on my door and my class was graduating. My parents were excited, asking if they should hire a bus for the ceremony, but I had to tell them I wasn't graduating yet because of some missed units. They understood; I think they knew it was too much, balancing school and the baby.

My dad was especially supportive when I mentioned I was thinking of leaving my boyfriend. I didn't tell him everything, but he just said, "If you need to come home, we'll be here."

I stopped by Nakuru with the nanny and baby on my way back home for Christmas, where my boyfriend had recently picked up a gig, earning about 100,000 Kenya shillings. He was bawling, he had hired a vehicle and he took me to Java on Christmas morning, the first proper date in five years of being together. But in my mind, I'd already decided—I was done with him. *This is the last time you're seeing me,* I thought. I went back to Kisii with the nanny and the baby, feeling like it was time to start fresh.

2017

I CAME BACK to Nairobi in January of 2017 without the baby. The Nakuru gig had ended, and my boyfriend was also back. I told him I left the baby in the village because we were trying to wean him off breast milk, and he ate it up.

My dad sent me 30,000 Kenya shillings, and I got a 13,000 shilling house in Ruaka. I didn't tell him I didn't have furniture. My parents had just retired, and I didn't want to bother them. Besides my job, I had started selling clothes. I would go to Gikomba Market, get clothes, and sell them to my friends. At the end of the month, it would come to around 6,000 shillings, so I was sure I could manage living on my own.

I moved on a Sunday. He had left me alone in the house, and I figured it was my chance. When he came back at 3:00 a.m., like he usually did, he would find only wind. I didn't want the neighbors to know I was moving out, so I had the taxi wait behind the house.

He came back at around 5:00 p.m., that evening as I was giving my things to the taxi guy. He wore a look of confusion. "Where are you going? I thought we had such a nice December, why are you leaving me?" He got on his knees and started crying. "You can't go like this. I'll make up for the rent and the deposit you've paid for the house in Ruaka. Just don't go. Don't leave me."

After all his crying, he started threatening me.

"You know I'm going to take that baby away from you. You can't go with my baby. You go and leave my baby here."

Even after his crying, begging, and threatening, I still left. I took the mattress which I had bought for 12,000 shillings, my clothes, the baby's clothes, and my books. I love my books—I had about 150 at that time.

I had spoken to my best friend's parents, who had a set of seats they were not using, and they agreed to sell them to me for 10,000 Kenya shillings. I went to their house, which was behind Garden City, got the sofas, and headed to Ruaka. I remember I spent that night in tears. The whole time I was questioning my decision. "Why would I be so stupid as to leave this man?"

He also spent the whole night calling and crying. "Where are you? I'm coming to get you now. There is no way you're going to leave me."

After two weeks, I got back the baby and the nanny. I could barely make ends meet, and to top it all off, I got fired from my job. My depression hit new heights. I used to put the baby to sleep, then sit and cry while praying. "What am I going to do? I don't have a degree to look for a job, and the transcripts I have are full of blanks."

There was a guy on Instagram who really liked my style. He had a boutique in town. He told me he would pay me 15,000 shillings, monthly to run three of his social media pages. He also told me I could go to his shop on Wednesdays and Fridays, and at the end of the week, he would pay me 1,000 shillings. It wasn't enough, but I was getting somewhere.

At this time, my boyfriend started reaching out. "Can I come and see the baby?" he would whimper, and I would let him. He usually came with a paper bag of bananas and oranges. "*Sasa ju hutaki maneno yangu*, you provide for the baby," he'd say whenever I asked if that was all he could manage, even though he knew I needed a little bit more than a bunch of bananas and five oranges.

When I was really pushed, I would call my dad crying, and ask him to send me some money. My dad felt I was really struggling and told me to take the baby back home while I tried to figure out my life. I took the baby and the nanny back home in April of 2017.

My social media gig started doing well. I opened an Instagram page and sold clothes online. Around my birthday in July, my boyfriend reached out again.

"Happy birthday," he said excitedly.

"Thank you." I kept the conversation short and ended things there.

Around August, I got a call from his grandmother who I had visited often because she lived in Kisii. "*Kwanini sijakuona?* What happened? *Nimekuja* Nairobi and I want to see you. When can you come and see me in Umoja?"

"I'm working from Monday to Saturday, but I think we can plan for Sunday," I told her.

I went to Umoja, where one of his aunt's lived, and I found his grandma and a bunch of his aunties waiting for me. They sat me down and started asking what happened. I told them about the infidelities and the abuse, and they didn't even flinch.

"That's how men are. *Ata mimi* immediately *niliolewa nilikuwa nachapwa*," one of them volunteered without being asked.

"You're not allowed to question when your man is coming back home. *Akitoka kwa nyumba hiyo ni shughuli yake. Hizo ndizo vitu zinafanya unachapwa*," another one fired.

"Just let him be. Don't bother going through his phone. His phone is his private property. Also, you're supposed to be cooking for your man. Whenever he comes home, make sure you have food ready," the first one continued.

"And don't warm his food, *ugali inafaa kuwa* fresh, fresh," the second aunt supported the first aunt's sentiments.

They didn't even believe me when I said he got violent. They thought it was just a light slap, and not something that would make me leave a marriage.

He later joined us, and that's when I realized it was an intervention. "I'm ready to take this woman back as long as she is ready to do what you have told her." The only thing I wanted was to bring my son back, and I thought it might work with him in the picture. "You can come back, but I don't want to see anything from your house. *Wewe kuja tu na nguo zako na za mtoto.*"

I went and sold the seats I had bought from my friend's parents for 3,000 Kenya shillings and used it to taxi my mattress, clothes, and books back to the staff SQ. I went back to Kisii and got the baby and our nanny. I didn't tell my parents I was getting back with my boyfriend. I told them two months after I moved back in with him, but my mom had sensed it.

"Are you sure you're not going back to that man?"

"Mom, *mi siendi kwake. Nataka tu kukaa na mtoto.*"

Every time I left my boyfriend, his financial situation got better. He was doing really well now. He decided that our family was growing, and it was time to move out of the staff SQ into a bigger house. He told me to go and look for a nice two-bedroom house in Utawala. He said he wanted to start afresh. We only carried our clothes, the carpet, gas cooker, mattress, and TV.

We moved to our two-bedroom house in September of 2017. In hindsight, that was the worst decision I ever made.

Utawala is at the end of the world. You go past the airport and you keep going into a sea of dust and empty fields. I tried to look on the brighter side; Life was getting better, we were moving to a two-bedroom house, I was earning some money, and he was doing well and had started a gaming shop with two TVs and two PlayStations. We were moving up.

Two months into moving, he started dropping the past into conversations. "Why would you leave me when I was struggling the most and take my son away? Did you think that was something I would ever forgive?" I brushed it off, thinking it wasn't a big deal. Whenever we had an argument, he would bring up the "You left me" conversation. I couldn't tell him he was the reason I left; I knew he wouldn't understand.

"You used to beat me up," I would sometimes say.

"I was making a point to show you how a wife should treat a husband. Now when I come home, you've cooked for me, when my friends come over, you treat them well, wash their hands, and make conversation, and they no longer say you're a snob. You should be thanking me. I have helped you grow into the woman you are today."

My depression got worse. My friends from Political Science and Philosophy started calling to ask if I was graduating. "We're just finishing up, *tunangoja tu* graduation." I would sit and tear up, wondering what I was doing with my life. *I know I have a baby, but I don't know whether that's the one achievement I wanted to be known for. I wanted to be a lawyer or a political scientist and at least take one degree back to my parents.*

To add salt to the wound, my boyfriend started monitoring my finances. He would take all my money and say something like, "My business needs a new PlayStation," or a new TV, or some fresh nonsense like that. "Be patient, I'm investing the money. You're going to see the fruits very soon," he would say. Afraid of his temper, I wouldn't push the issue further.

Pregnant

AT THE END of October, I found out I was pregnant. I didn't tell him because I was still deciding if I wanted to be in a relationship with him. The pregnancy, my disrupted studies, and the fact that I was working while he kept all the money pushed me into total darkness. I dissociated from things. I stopped looking for my grades in school. The only thing I cared about was my son. Nothing else made sense.

I stopped talking to my boyfriend. I didn't want to have sex with him either, but when I refused, he would force himself on me. I couldn't leave because I had no savings. The tension was so thick that we'd speak to each other through the nanny or the baby. *Ambia daddy. Ambia mommy.*

He would come home anytime between 11:00 p.m., and 3:00 a.m., and still expect me to wake up and cook. He had started a *kinyozi* in Mukuru kwa Rueben and would come home drunk, saying he was hustling for us. "I'm not formally employed, so I have to hustle till late." I started resenting him, silently building anger because I was afraid of confronting him.

Once, he came home around 11:30 p.m., drunk. I usually had to go downstairs to open the gate for him since he refused to get a key, claiming it was my "wifely duty." After we got inside, he demanded food.

I'd grown up in a home where if my dad came home late, my mom wouldn't bother; it was generally up to him to sort himself out. I'd told my boyfriend this, and he'd snapped, "*Ni kwa sababu mama yako ni mkamba. Kwa wakisii* we don't do that."

This night, I told him I had a headache and couldn't make him food but there were leftovers he could warm up. He went to the kitchen in silence, warmed his food, ate, and came to bed. I thought I'd won and decided I'd start standing up for myself more.

I did the same the next night, and again he quietly warmed his food, ate, and came to bed. When he asked for sex, I said no, and he kept quiet and slept. The next morning after he showered, I did not wash his dirty boxers and he did it himself. I kept this up for about two weeks, feeling like I was winning this battle. I didn't know he was talking to his aunt, complaining about how I wouldn't cook or wash his clothes, making him do these things himself.

I decided I didn't want to be in a relationship with him anymore. I couldn't imagine being yoked to him forever with a second baby. So I resolved to terminate my pregnancy, the same way I had done in my hostel days with Cytotec, Misoprostol. A quack doctor I knew on River Road was willing to sell me the pills for 5,000 Kenya shillings. I called a friend for a loan, but after getting the pills, I suddenly became unsure and I put them away, not knowing they would come back to haunt me.

Everything unraveled one morning around 10:00 a.m. The nanny was on the rooftop doing laundry, and my son had woken up. He usually said, "Mom, *nataka beebix*." And I'd sit him on his little plastic seat, put on some cartoons, and feed him Weetabix.

My boyfriend woke up at around 9:30 a.m., showered, and went to the bedroom, expecting me to have laid out clean, ironed clothes for him. With the confidence I'd found in standing up for myself, I'd neglected that duty too. I mean, what was he going to do about it besides quietly do it himself?

He came to the living room in a towel, asking, "*Mama Ed, why aren't my clothes laid out?*" I stayed silent. "I'm talking to you. *Mbona unaninyamazia? Ni nini mbaya na wewe?*"

He went back to the bedroom, and I thought I'd won again. But he returned to the living room dressed in his dirty boxers, shorts and a t-shirt, locked the door, and put the key in his pocket. I was following him from the corner of my eye, and when he locked the door with a padlock I realized, "Oh shit, I'm in trouble. Fuck! Why didn't I just do what this guy was telling me? Why did I push him?"

He took me by my foot and dragged me from the living room to our bedroom, locking the bedroom door and pocketing the key. "*Sasa leo* you're going to understand that you're not the man in this house. You're going to know that not talking to me, answering me back, and denying me sex will cost you."

He'd found the Cytotec pills and assumed I'd already aborted. He unplugged the extension cord, wrapped the cable around it, and started bringing it down on me until it broke. Then he cut the cable, using it to whip me. He threw me against the wall and then started kicking and punching me wherever his foot or fist would reach. It didn't matter if it was my face, stomach or legs. If he wasn't kicking or punching me, he was whipping me with the cable he was holding. I have never been so scared for my life the way I was that day.

When he started kicking my stomach, I cried, "Do you know I'm pregnant? You're hurting the baby."

"So now you're finally telling me you're pregnant? You think I don't know you've already taken the pills and aborted? You're a witch. You won't kill me like you killed my baby."

He took the cable, wrapped it around my neck and started choking me. He choked me till my eyes bulged out of my head and I started feeling dizzy before letting go, and then did it again. "Scream as much as you want. Do you think anyone is coming here to help you? You're going to die here and no one is going to do shit about it. I'm going to take my baby and move to another country. I will leave you in this house and you will rot."

He went and got his belt and used it to choke me to the point where I was passing out and then he let go. "You see what you've made me do," he kept telling me. "You want to give me stress till I die. I am too young to die so I'm going to show you I'm the man in this house and you're not the boss of me, okay?"

My son, sensing something was wrong, knocked on the door, calling, "*Mama, mama*." My boyfriend opened the door and let him in. When he saw me crying, my son started crying too.

"You want to be a sissy now. You're going to be crying because your mom is crying? I am going to teach you to be a man. You can't be crying like your stupid mother here."

After letting my son in, my boyfriend prepared to leave the house. He went to the bathroom, so I took the keys from his shorts, unlocked the door and ran to a field somewhere, and sat there and cried. That's when my stomach started hurting, and I realized the baby was hurt. I sat there for about two hours and then headed back, telling myself, "By now he should have left the house." When I got there, the gate was locked, and I had to wait for a neighbor to open it.

The house was locked too. I went to the shop downstairs and told the woman there that I locked my phone together with my keys inside my house, and asked if she could help me by letting me use her phone to call for help. I called my dad. I didn't tell him I had just been beaten; I told him we had an argument, he'd locked the door, taken the baby, and I didn't know where they were. He tried to call him; my mom tried to call him too, but he wasn't picking up his phone.

I called the caretaker and fed him the same story about locking my keys inside. He came back with a padlock cutter. It was now three in the afternoon. A friend of my boyfriend's came and found me outside the house, trying to open the door. He asked what happened, and I told him that I had left my keys inside.

"And where is your boyfriend?" he asked.

"I don't know where he is." My plan was to open the door, get my phone, try to find out where my baby was, and leave.

This friend of his called him and told him, "*Nimeona mama anatry kuvunja mlango. Kwani ni nini inaendelea?*" My boyfriend came back a few minutes after the call.

"*Niko na ufunguo. Tuko sawa,*" he told the caretaker and opened the door.

We got into the house. The whole time he was not talking to me. "*Kwani* where did you take the baby?"

"*Si* you ran and left the baby in the house? That is not your concern. Just know the baby is safe." Being scared for my life, I didn't push him. I let it go. As long as the baby was fine, I would be fine. Plus, my dad had called the nanny and talked to the baby.

I started feeling excruciating pain in my stomach on Tuesday around midnight, two days after he had beaten me up. The pain was so intense that I woke him up and told him I thought I was dying. He rushed me to a nearby clinic. The doctor gave me morphine because I was in so much pain. I think this was the time the miscarriage was happening.

"Your wife was pregnant, but she's lost the baby," the doctor told my boyfriend. He advised us to get an ultrasound to check if the miscarriage was complete or if I needed a cleaning procedure. We did the ultrasound, and the doctor told us to wait two weeks. After I was done bleeding, we would do another ultrasound to make sure everything was clear.

After that, my boyfriend began probing about what happened. I told him I hadn't taken any Cytotec pills, but he didn't believe me. "I found those things in this house. Even if you didn't take them, it means you were thinking about getting rid of my child."

I tried to be subservient even while in pain. He would get home, and I'd serve him. On the Friday of the second week after the miscarriage, he came home drunk again. He didn't demand anything. He just came in, got into bed, and slept. The following morning, he woke up and started questioning the pregnancy. "If it was mine, why were you trying to get rid of it?" I stayed silent in an effort not to anger him. Again, he locked the door and put the key in his pocket. This time, I knew my parents would find me in City Mortuary. I said my last prayers, asked God for forgiveness, and told Him to take care of my son.

He took the plastic baby chair and started hitting me with it until it broke. He threw it away and started picking up shoes from the floor to hit me with, saying "You're being very fishy. You're not really telling me the truth about what happened. You're going to tell me the truth, or I'm going to kill you. That *kalittle* job of yours, from today I don't ever want to see you going to town. I want you to stay at home and take care of our son. *Hawa watu unakutana nao huko* town are putting ideas into your head. If you want money to go to the market, I'll give you money. This stupid job of yours, I never want to hear about it ever again."

He had a tool in the house for design, similar to a wall drill. After raining blows on me, he took it, plugged it in, and told me to kneel in front of him. The drill was spinning and spinning. I just felt my bladder let loose as urine trickled down my thigh and pooled on the floor.

He gave me a notebook and told me to write down five reasons why he shouldn't kill me. "You're going to tell me how you'll be a better wife. You're going to tell me how you'll be a better mom. And from today, you're going to be a housewife. I don't ever want to hear that you went to town again." I can't remember what I wrote down, but they added up to five.

"You're going to swear upon this. *Si* you're a lawyer? Swear upon this." He showed me where to sign and where to leave space for a witness. "If you go against what you've written, just know I'm going to kill you, and I'm going to take the baby from you." Already, I hadn't seen the baby in two weeks, so I knew he wasn't bluffing.

After I signed the "contract", he told me to stretch out my leg. "Have you sworn that you're not going to go to work ever again?" I nodded rapidly, hicupping "yes".

"Are you sure? Because I'm going to drill through your leg and you'll never walk again in your life, and I'll take you to the hospital in the afternoon *na ntasema ulianguka kwa* stairs."

"I swear I'm not going to work again," I said, shaking. "I'm just going to be a good wife and a good mother."

"I want you to be pregnant by next January. I don't know how you'll do it, but I want you to be pregnant so you can stay at home and take care of your kids."

I swore and begged him to unplug the drill. He finally did and then fetched his belt. And it was back to choking. I had no fight left in me. He choked me until I passed out. When I regained consciousness, he was towering above me still holding his belt. "Do you think you've had enough, or do you want me to continue?"

"I have had enough," I whimpered.

"I want you to wake up tomorrow morning, go to your aunt's place, show her this contract, and tell her you're going to be a good wife. I've been telling her what you've been doing to me. Go and tell her, and make sure *amesign hapa kwa* witness."

Even when he was beating me up and threatening me, he was completely turned on. He was wearing his boxers and you could see his manhood pressed against them, almost tearing a hole through them. I think power was a fetish for him. The fact that he was holding my life in his hands turned him on to dizzying heights.

"You've been starving me for too long, and I want sex now, okay?" he said. I told him I didn't think I was in a position to have sex, but he wasn't listening. "You spread your legs. I don't care what you're feeling or what's going on."

He finished within minutes. After he was done, he told me to clean myself up, saying my baby and the nanny were with his aunt, and I could go pick them up.

After he left, I called my dad. "He's told me where the baby is, but I think I'm done with him." I didn't tell him my boyfriend had been beating me up, fearing it would make things worse. He had told me if I ever spoke to my dad about anything going on in our house, he would kill me.

My dad asked how much money I had; I told him I had about 1,500 shillings on M-Pesa. In reality, I had nothing, but I told him that to soften the blow. He said he would try to get some money to me so that the next morning, I could get the baby, and go back to Kisii. "You don't have to carry anything from that house; just leave." The next day, he sent me 3,000 Kenya shillings, and my boyfriend left me 200 shillings, just enough to get to his aunt's place and back.

I called my best friend and told her how badly I'd been beaten up by my boyfriend. My thighs were bloody. My eyes were swollen shut. I looked so bad I couldn't even leave the house without people asking questions. She said she'd talk to her mom, get her car, and come pick me up in the morning. All I needed to do was make sure my boyfriend was not around.

On Saturday, I went to his aunt's place wearing my long-sleeved blouse. My eyes were not as puffy. His aunt began questioning me. "*Kwa nini unapatia mtoto wetu* stress? Why don't you want to be a good wife? Marriages *ni kuvumiliana.*

You can't be telling him you're going to leave him every time you have an argument. *Kupika tu ndiyo inakushinda?*"

I took the baby and the nanny, then called my friend. I only took three suitcases—mine, my son's, and the nanny's—and carried the books I really liked. Two Harry Potter novels and a Steve Berry novel, and that was it.

There is another friend of mine who lived in Kahawa. She happened to have gone to visit their folks in Eldoret for the Christmas holidays. She told me I could take my suitcases there, and stay for a while. She even instructed her brother to wait for me. The house had been locked because they hadn't paid rent, and they hadn't even paid for electricity. We bribed the caretaker, and he opened the door for us. I stayed at my friend's house, and the next day we went to Kisii. My boyfriend didn't try to reach out—not once.

2018

ON DECEMBER 31ST, 2017, I decided to come back to Nairobi. I didn't have anything to do in the village, so I left my son with the nanny and returned. I went back to the house in Kahawa. I woke up in the New Year on my own and I switched off the phone. The depression was 10 times heavier. I felt so worthless. I felt I couldn't go on. I had told my parents I had come back to finish my studies, but in reality, I had come to finish myself.

At around three o'clock in the afternoon, I left the house to take a walk. There was a chemist nearby. I went in and told the chemist I had a really bad migraine and, could he recommend a strong painkiller. He suggested a 50 shilling painkiller. I told him to give me painkillers worth 500 Kenya shillings. I went back to the house and locked myself in, thinking that was my last day on earth.

I didn't see the point of living anymore. The abortions and the miscarriage I'd had made me feel like the worst person on earth. On top of that, the emotional and physical abuse and the fact that I had quit my job and I was broke were making me feel miserable. How could I let my parents raise my son? They were retired; they should be relaxed, not troubled by my trivial affairs.

When I got back to the house, I switched on my phone, and found that no one had called me. I found it absurd that even when I was about to kill myself, the world was moving on, and no one cared that I was going through hell. I felt so alone. I went and got a glass of water, contemplating how many pills I would need to take to sleep forever.

I had 10 pills and I decided they wouldn't be enough. I had a bit of money—my dad had given me 5,000 Kenya shillings when I left home. I decided I would send my nanny 3,000 shillings, then use the remaining cash to go to two different chemists and get more pills. I sent my nanny the money and left the house. As I was walking, my phone started ringing. It was the guy whose social media accounts I used to run. I wondered why he was disturbing me and ignored the call. He called again. I ignored. He called yet again, and this time I picked up.

"Happy New Year. *Nimekumiss. Kwani uko wapi?*" he said jubilantly.

"*Niko tu* Nairobi."

"*Si* you come and see me in the morning? There is something I want to talk to you about."

I didn't go to the chemist after all. I decided to go and hear what he had to say. Maybe he was giving me some cash; after all, he owed me some money. I could use it to cover the nanny's salary for about six months, and my parents wouldn't have to struggle as much.

The next morning, I went to see him. He told me the guy who was working for him had quit, and he was thinking that, since I had a child, I could use the job. I thought this was the thing I needed to hold on to—like that saving grace. I felt there was something in the universe that must have been working. There was no way this guy called me out of the blue and someone quit their job just when I was at my lowest point. I felt, yeah, maybe I was still needed on this earth for something.

I stayed with my friend in Kahawa, who by then, had paid the rent for her house. I didn't ask my dad to loan me any money; it was enough that I had left the baby with them. I worked for the guy for that month and managed to save 15,000 Kenya shillings. My friend helped me get a small bedsitter for 6,000 shillings and gave me a mattress, a blanket, one bedsheet, and a pillow. Her place was walking distance from mine. After work, I would go back to her place, have a meal, and then walk back to my place.

My house was depressing. It was on the ground floor, when it rained, water seeped in through the door. It smelled musty and there was mold growing on the walls. One night, it rained so heavily that the house flooded to the point where my carpet and mattress were soaking. I took two suitcases, joined them together, placed clothes on top, and slept on them.

Six months into 2018, during my birthday, my boyfriend contacted me through the aunt who lived in Utawala. "Happy birthday. *Unajua nimekumbuka ni* birthday *yako* because my son's birthday also falls on the same date. *Si* you come I take you out tomorrow." The next day was Saturday, so I obliged. I wasn't expecting the same intervention that had happened before would happen again.

After staying at her house for a bit, we went to a nearby hotel, she said she would buy me a glass of wine, and I could tell her what has been happening in my life after I left their child. I told her how much he abused me and she started crying. "He's coming here to see you; I'm sorry, it was his idea." I was in denial and told her I had healed and it was okay.

"*Mama* Ed, you're glowing. *Kwani* what have you been doing to yourself all this time we haven't been together?" he said when he got to our table. "*Si* you just give me a hug." He behaved as if nothing happened, as if it was my fault that we were not on speaking terms.

His aunt excused herself. "*Time imeenda sana, wacha nikaangalie watoto.* By the way, he's driving now. *Atakudrop tu* home, don't worry about it." Since I had had like three glasses of wine, I went with it.

He apologized. "I'm really sorry about what happened last year, but there's also something I want to ask you." He went back to my miscarriage. I don't think he will ever accept that he was the one who caused it. He has convinced himself that I took the pills.

Since he's the father of my child, I knew I would have to put up with him. Regardless of how I felt, I knew I would have to be friendly and cordial towards him.

I went and got my son and the nanny from Kisii in October. By this time, my boyfriend had moved in with another girl. He got into this habit of drunk-dialing me every Friday evening. He would then come over to my house, we would have sex, and then he would go back to his house. I didn't know how to end it. I still felt I needed to be friendly with him for our son's sake, and sometimes I was lonely, so I thought, *Let me tolerate him and sweep every terrible thing he's done under the rug.*

His girlfriend started calling. "Now you, you left this guy, and you want to take him from me? Stop being a whore and let him move on with his life."

When he picked our child for the weekend, the girlfriend would take photos of herself with my son and send them to me. "See how your son loves me? We're going to get married and be a family." And I would sit there bitter, thinking, *I'm just tolerating your boyfriend because I need him to start pulling his weight.*

He called me one drunken night in December of 2018. "You know, I've been thinking a lot about you, and I think I want you back in my life. Even that girl who used to text you—I've chased her out of my house, and I want you to come back."

"I will be so happy to come back," I told him, not knowing where my head was.

When I went home for the December holidays, he told me not to return to Nairobi with the baby because he wanted us to sit down and talk. I was really excited. I had no idea why. When I got back, he called me and took me out for coffee.

He told me he loved me but was at a point in his life where he needed to be on his own. "I've thought about taking you back, and I don't want to do this just because of the baby. I need space to grow on my own. If we're meant to be, we'll end up together, and if not, we'll just co-parent." He was doing so well, and I felt I deserved to benefit from that. I was already building sandcastles of us going on holidays together. So when he finished his speech, I was heartbroken.

2019

I HAD BEEN saving for some time. Toward the end of December 2018, I moved out of the bedsitter to another one.

The fact that we didn't get back together, I feel, made me a better person. Since then, my business has been thriving. I've gotten a lot of styling, video and photoshoot gigs. In April, I moved into a one-bedroom house and went all out and decked out the entire space.

After I settled in, I went home and brought the baby back—I had sent him to Kisii to visit his grandparents for the holidays. My ex-boyfriend used to call me every now and then, so this time, when he called, I told him someone wanted to talk to him and gave my son the phone. "*Kwani*, the baby came? Where are you? I want to come and see him," he said after he finished talking to our son. I gave him my address, and he came immediately.

After seeing how well I'm doing, he now comes up with all sorts of antics to see me. The other day, he told me he wanted to take me out for coffee because his life was in danger and, since I'm a lawyer, I could tell him what to do.

"People have been calling me and threatening my life," he tells me without getting into details.

A day later, he calls and says he didn't want to tell me because his phone is bugged and asks if we can meet again. This time, he has a fresh story. "There is this woman I've been sleeping with, and I didn't know she was married. Now her husband wants to kill me. I drove her car to Kisii to see our baby without knowing it was also bugged. Now the husband knows we have a kid, and he's coming for all of us. That's why I'm so concerned. Even when I call you at night, it's because

I want to know if there's something fishy going on around you."

When it's not scare tactics, it's drunk dialing. He calls me in the middle of the night to profess his love for me. "I love you so much that I can't do this life without you. Our son needs us to be together." Twice or three times a month, he comes to my house around 1:00 a.m., honks his car horn until I open the gate, then starts crying, asking why I won't take him back when I know he can give our son a better life. I let him sleep on the couch, and after some time, he wakes up and comes into my bed, sleeping there until morning.

I told him I didn't feel safe when he comes around, and he told me he's a changed man, that he'd started going to church. "I will never raise my hand against a woman ever again," he vows. We haven't been intimate at all in 2019, but some days, I feel weak and want to give in. Then I remember the man he is and snap out of it. Besides, at the end of last year, his ex-girlfriend texted me to tell me he had beaten her like a dog, and she was in hospital.

Since the inking of this story, a therapist reached out and volunteered to take her case on a pro-bono basis. The weight of her past is slowly becoming lighter with every sunset and her future a little brighter with every sunrise.

Don't grow to be cynical
continue to believe
in the magic of the world
in the magic of people
in the magic of love

Acknowledgments

Many things have had to fall into place for this book to be seated on your hands, and I consider that a miracle. The conception of these stories began when I started my blog *Kisauti* in 2016 and they have been birthed in 2024. A couple of people have been the midwives of this book.

Eunniah Mbabazi, my copy editor, who filled the book with red when I thought it was ready, and I had to sit for another six months making the changes. Every red mark a beam that has made the stories in this book stand even taller.

M. Ruiyot, polished the book even further, making it sparkle, and making me wonder if I should put it on a bookshelf or frame it on my wall, only to realize I could do both.

Stephen Njogu, who has been the cover designer for both *Drug Paradise* and *The Sponsor,* came through for *Imperfect Match* yet again. It is always a pleasure working with him. It astonishes me how I give him a dull, incoherent concept, and he comes back with fireworks every time.

Honorable mentions to John Babu, for doing the illustration of the book in the blink of an eye; Charles Chanchori, my fellow author who has a background in law; and Mary Gichira, my Legal Counsel and Advocate of the High Court of Kenya, for their wisdom on criminal law, that has helped improve the quality of this book.

Special thanks to my friends and family for always supporting and believing in this journey that I am on, to the people who have opened themselves up and trusted me with their stories, and to you, dear reader, for always being ready and willing to turn the page on my work.

None of this is lost on me.

For this and everything you keep giving me,

shukran!

If You Enjoyed This…

If you enjoyed *Imperfect Match*, take one minute to spread the word in the form of a short review on your social sites or a whisper to a friend or two. I will be thankful, and new readers will be too.

K. Kimuyu is a writer based in Nairobi. When he is not writing novels, short stories and poems, he is consulting for some of the biggest brands in the country. He has had this pull into the literary and advertising world for the longest time and he finally decided to give into both.

His dream to be a writer started as a smolder, to touch people with words the way words have touched him and it's growing into a fire. He is struck every time he receives messages from readers loving his books and asking when the next one will be out.

He has vowed (in front of his house mirror) that he will always have a new book for his readers every year. The next one is *Kesho & Malkia,* set to come out in 2025. His timelines can be shaky. Find him on his social pages—@wakimuyu on Instagram, Facebook, and X—so you can pester him, just in case he forgets and an year turns into two.

Coming Soon

KESHO & MALKIA
Divided by Misfortune, Brought Together by Blood

Turn page to read preview...

The Prostitute

Malkia usually opened her business at midnight. That was when her clients were bold enough to come out and play. There was something about the sun going down and the moon coming up that awakened a man's lustful urge. She usually passed via Sunfood Chicken and Chips and ate supper before heading to her corner on Koinange Street. Today, she was running late and decided to have the chicken and chips packed, to eat on the streets as she awaited her clients.

"Chips *funga amekuja na* chips *funga*," Daniela, a plump girl in a black, short minidress chortled in between, smoking her cigarette, and giggling when she saw Malkia opening her bag of fries and chicken.

"Mchoyo anakula peke yake," Yvonne, a tall girl in a pink wig, pink miniskirt, and purple platform heels got close to Malkia, picking four sticks of fries. *"Uchoyo itakumaliza,"* she added, chewing loudly, and pinching a big piece of chicken from Malkia's bag.

"Siko hapa kukulea," Malkia said, turning the bag away from her.

"Wewe hata kujilea umeshindwa, utanilea?" Yvonne barked.

Malkia ignored her and continued eating her supper. After she was done, she folded the bag and made to throw it away. A body stirred in the corner of the street. Brown eyes burned like a touch in the dim light. The rest of the body was hidden in a dirty *gunia.*

"Usitupe," a boy's voice cracked. He could not be any older than 10, Malkia thought, and instantly felt sadness embrace her like the cold.

"Zimebaki chipo tatu zimeungua na mifupa."

"Nipatie. Ziko sawa hivyo."

Malkia inched closer and squatted next to him. Her blue micro-mini skirt peeled up her thighs to the size of her belt as she did, exposing her white panties. She gave him the bag and proceeded to watch him clear the fries, and clean the scanty meat on the bones—his teeth digging into them, turning the bones to shreds within seconds. She looked at him keenly. His brown eyes bore into her, and reminded her of someone familiar. Had she seen this boy before? She wondered—her mind drawing a blank.

"*Naitwa* Malkia, *unaitwa nani*?" she asked.

"*Kesho*," the boy said, averting his gaze from hers.

Malkia got up and smoothed her skirt, and started walking back towards Daniela and Yvonne.

"*Asante*," Kesho murmured.

Malkia stopped momentarily. "*Karibu*," she said. The words catching in her throat for a split second before she joined her group.

"Malkia, *nani amekuhuzunisha*?" Yvonne asked loudly.

"Ah, *ni chokora tu.*"

"*Ni ule pale, tumfunze adabu sahii?*"

"*Wachana na yeye, hana* story."

Malkia took the cigarette stick from Daniela's fingers, and gave it three puffs before returning it to her. "*Hawa chokora wamekuwa wengi sana,*" Yvonne continued absentmindedly, applying lipstick and smacking her lips together as Malkia reached into her handbag, and popped chewing gum in her mouth—that same handbag that had pepper spray and a penknife for protection.

They had both hated her when she first came to Koinange Street. Being younger and comelier than all of them, they had been fiercely jealous of her. '*Wewe malaya, rudi kule umetoka. Hizi* streets *zina wenyewe.*'

Yvonne being tall with masculine features that not even tiny skirts and feminine colors could water down, had fought her after she took her biggest client on her first night on the street. "*Ntakuharibu hii sura tuone ni mwanaume mgani atakutaka.*" She had kicked, slapped, punched, and scratched her face, leaving it blooded with marks that took almost three months to heal. But that did not keep her from coming back to the streets, and even with her swollen face, men preferred her to the others.

"*Wewe Malaya, hiyo kuma yako umeweka nini, juju? Tutakuja na makasi tukurarue hadi kwa tumbo,*" Daniela yelled one night.

"*Hata ukirarua hadi kwa mdomo, wanaume watanichagua wakuache hapo tu,*" she had fired.

Yvonne had snorted out a loud laugh, Daniela followed, and they were all soon laughing. That's how their camaraderie began.

Malkia took the lipstick from Yvonne, applied it on her lips and smacked them together. "*Siko hapa kukulea,*" Yvonne smirked, snatched it from her hands, and put it back in her handbag.

Malkia turned around and looked at Kesho. He was first asleep in his *gunia*. The site made sadness embrace her once more. She decided she would be having her supper on the street, and sharing it with the boy from then onwards and maybe they too could begin building a camaraderie of their own.

Her Clients

When Kesho was asleep, Malkia was busy. A graying man with a sturdy stature wearing a colorful suit held her hand and took her behind a dingy aisle. His colorful pants dropped around his ankles, and Malkia dropped on her knees. They were there for three minutes before Malkia came out wiping the white on her mouth, and counting her money.

A young gentleman came along. He looked like a teenager. But Malkia could tell that he was in his late 20s. Sometimes, he hated the way men aged. You only started knowing their age when they were approaching their 40s, and even then you had a hard time putting your finger on it. It behooved her to know their age, it was a window, albeit a small one into how experienced they were, and how she needed to handle them.

The young gentleman introduced himself, and began asking about her hobbies and favorite color. "When you're paying, you can skip that part," Malkia said while taking his hand. "My favorite color is blue," she added, leading him to a nearby lodging. She came back with three crisp 1,000 shilling notes, and readjusted her favorite color to brown while touching up her makeup and lipstick.

Two girls came along and they disappeared into the same lodging. Girls were always fun. Malkia loved the kissing, finger-play and how free she felt with women because she could truly let her guard down. The two women were sensual lesbians, new in town, looking for a good time. After an hour of heavy petting, kissing, playing with toys, and smoking marijuana, Malkia came out counting her money, smoothing her dress, and touching up her makeup.

The hour hand was touching 3:00 a.m. She had made good money tonight. She decided she would take two more clients, and head home. Before she could have another thought, a Toyota Sientra flashed its lights, and she ran towards it. Inside was a man who appeared to be in his mid-40s. He introduced himself as Dave, and to her surprise they pulled into a Five Star hotel.

Malkia got to observe him properly as they sat down in the hotel's restaurant to have dinner—he was tall with a paunch. He had a look that said he was in management, and he made a good living.

"Tell me Malkia, what is a pretty girl like you, doing in a job like this?" Dave asked, putting afire a cigar, and tapping the tip on a cigarette dish.

"I like it. It has flexible hours," Malkia tried to make him laugh as their food arrived. It was the first time she had been to a five-star hotel, and more than anything she wanted to impress him with her order. She had gone on to order things she didn't know, things she had only read in novels—fried prawns, jacket potatoes with a side of sweet corn soup, and a glass of Sauvignon Blanc.

"What do your family members think about your line of work?" Dave asked, having put off his cigar, and now tearing into his goat ribs.

"My parents and siblings are a story I would rather not bore you with," Malkia said, forking a jacket potato together with a piece of prawn, and dipping it into the sweet corn soup. "You already know what I do and I know nothing about you? You could as well be a serial killer?" she added to change the topic.

"Sorry to disappoint you. I am just a boring tourist from Uganda, here to try your nyama choma," Dave said, dropping a clean bone on his plate."

"So you're just here for nyama choma?"

"Uhuh."

"And how is it."

"I am not complaining," he said, holding Malkia's gaze for almost a minute.

It had been long since Malkia had been wined and dined, and it was getting her hot under the collar. "What do you say we take this somewhere private, so I can give you dessert?"

Dave winked and led the way to his hotel room. The door had barely clicked behind them before they started kissing. Malkia loved how she had to tip-toe to get to his lips, and how his big hands grabbed her tiny waist. She pushed him and he fell on the king-size bed, and Malkia took him in her mouth. She was dripping and gasping when she had barely begun. She reached into her purse took out a condom and got on top of him.

"I am astonished the bed is still standing," Dave gasped after they were done.

Malkia remained silent, she could get used to this, she thought while sipping on the whiskey that had been brought by room service.

"You should be my wife," Dave groaned.

"A big man like you doesn't have a wife?" Malkia asked and realized that she was not only referring to how she perceived him as a man, but also to what was behind the zip of his trousers.

"I haven't had much luck with love," he responded.

"Why is that?"

He went silent. It was a question even Malkia couldn't answer herself. "We all need different things, and it's rare to come across someone who fulfills them all. When the sex works, they are emotionally unavailable. When they are emotionally available, they hate their mother," Malkia said, and grinned.

"You see, you get me," Dave said, putting his arm around her.

"How long are you staying here?"

"I'm here for two weeks."

Malkia's lifestyle for the two weeks flashed in front of her face, and she gleamed. "That's plenty of time to be your wife," she said, snuggling further into his arm.

They cuddled and talked until they fell asleep.

Malkia woke up in the morning, and Dave was not beside her. *Perhaps he's gone to have breakfast,* she thought and jumped in the shower.

After the shower, Dave was still nowhere to be seen. She opened the drawers and looked around the table, but he had not left the fee of 25,000 Kenya shillings they had agreed on. The most she found was a picture of him, next to a woman and three smiling kids who looked like a photocopy of him. "Why lie to a prostitute?" Malkia muttered under her breath.

She got dressed, touched up her makeup, and went to have breakfast. There were different types of bread and soups. Malkia fixed herself a bowl of mushroom soup and a croissant. She wiped her plate clean and went back for two sausages, two eggs, French beans, and bacon with a glass of orange juice. She finished off her breakfast with slices of watermelon and pineapples, then went to the reception area where she found a smiling receptionist. The smile was less cordial but more knowing.

"I'm with Dave. He's here for two weeks. He will be taking care of my bills," Malkia said with the slightest hint of pomposity in her tone.

"Dave? The receptionist raised her brow as if that was not his real name. "Are you referring to the gentleman you came with yesterday?"

Malkia nodded.

"I'm afraid he has already checked out."

"Did he leave any cash for his companion?" Malkia asked.

She smiled again. "No, he was here for a business conference. His bill was already paid for by the company.

"Can you give me his contacts?" Malkia was already thinking of a few not-so-flowery words to tell him.

"That is not possible. We don't disclose our client's details."

"Okay," Malkia said and started leaving.

"Miss, one more thing. The receptionist said, typing on her computer. "Here is the bill for your stay," she said extending a receipt.

The blood drained from Malkia's face. She took the receipt ready to protest but then, all that was there was the supper and breakfast she had eaten, and the alcohol she had indulged in, the only problem was that they totaled 8,000 Kenya shillings. All the money she had made that night. She dug into her brazier, and paid apprehensively.

"I hope you enjoyed your stay and you will come back again," the receptionist said, smiling for the third time as Malkia raced out of the hotel, before they could give her another bill.

275

Her Friend

Kesho was woken up by the hooting of cars, opening of shops, cleaning of floors, and cold water seeping into his makeshift bedroom. He got up, folded his torn, dirty blanket, and stuffed it into his now wet *gunia*. He then got his bottle of gum and sniffed it; it helped kill the pangs of hunger if only for a bit.

He staggered into the road, and a speeding *matatu* missed him by a hair.

"*Wewe chokora angalia kwenye unaenda,*" the *makanga* barked. Kesho stabbed his middle finger in the air, straightened up, and started walking towards Gikomba market. Sometimes he got some work ferrying sacks of potatoes, tomatoes, or bales of clothes from one point to another and received a plate of hot food or some money to buy a meal in exchange.

But most times, he got sneers and jeers and eyes that told him that he was not welcome there.

"*Wewe chokora hiyo kinyasa uliiba wapi?*" a vendor chirped as he passed.

"*Hakuna kazi ya chokora hapa,*" another one roared.

A lady garbed in what looked like an expensive sweater, with a face full of makeup and a weave touching her back, wrinkled her nose before closing her nostrils with her thumb and forefinger as he passed by.

"*Hiyo maringo peleka* uptown," someone shouted. Kesho only realized the voice was beside him when someone grabbed his arm; a shabby guy whose face radiated with street smarts. "*Kuna kazi,*" he told Kesho, still holding his arm while using his other hand to hold a *manadazi.* "*Enda uongee na* Johnte, *ule chali mrefu mnono anapiga* story *pale,*" he let go of his arm and pointed at an M-Pesa shop. "*Mwambie ni* Timo *amekutuma,*" he said finally as he bit into his *mandazi.*

"*Unataka nini hapa?*" Johnte said with an edge to his tone as if he had been removed from something important.

"*Nimetumwa na* Timo, *amenishow kuna job?*" Kesho continued, realizing there was a lady in the M-Pesa shop who was all smiles.

"*Oh, sawa. Ngoja hapo dakika mbili.*" Kesho stood there rooted to the spot. "*Si kwa uso yangu,*" Johnte barked, and Kesho moved back four paces.

He stood there and watched Johnte giggling and laughing with the M-Pesa lady for almost half an hour before he joined him. "*Heh, bado ukohapa? Haya, nifuate.*" He took him to the public pit latrines around the corner and gave him a tin bucket with a string. Flies buzzed everywhere, and even Kesho couldn't help but wrinkle his nose the way the uptown lady had done.

"*Umewaifanya kazi ya* sewage?" Johnte asked, and Kesho shook his head sideways, already dreading the answer that would follow.

"*Usijali, haina kisomo. Unaingiza hii ndoo ndani ya choo, unachota asali, alufu unamwaga kwa zile drums ziko pale. Timo atakuja na mkokoteni aenda kuzimwaga* Nairobi River *masaa yake.*"

"*Na pesa?*"

"*Tutaongea ukimaliza.*"

Kesho smelled like rotten eggs after the drums were full, and his purple shorts were muddied with shit stains. He went back to the M-Pesa shop to look for Johnte and Timo. "*Wewe chokora enda ukaoge,*" the lady in the shop said, annoyed. You could not have said she was the one who had been all smiles earlier. "*Ati* Johnte? *Kamtafute kwa bafu,*" she added dismissively.

Darkness was almost falling; Kesho had searched for Timo and Johnte in every corner of Gikomba, but they were nowhere to be found. He decided to go and rummage Nation Centre's dustbins for leftover food, containers to sell, or both, and look for Timo and Johnte in the morning.

He got to Nation Centre at around 10:00 p.m., and stuck his head in the first dustbin he came across. He found a bottle of pineapple juice that was half-full and a spoiled sandwich full of ants. He brushed the ants aside and gobbled the sandwich in one bite. He washed it down with the juice and got back to the bin.

Today was his lucky day, he thought, after coming across three empty water bottles, an empty can of soda, and two empty plastic takeaway dishes. He started stuffing them into his *gunia*, and then he was running while holding his oversized purple shorts full of shit stains to keep them from falling.

"*Wewe chokora ntakuambia mara ngapi sitaki kukuona hapa?*" The thin guard with a fat *rungu* was hot on his heels.

He jumped a pothole and entered a deserted alley. Squeezed in between two parked minibuses, and he was out of sight. He got to his spot on Koinange Street when it was approaching midnight. He removed his blanket and made his bed using the containers as his pillow. He cozied up. His stomach was still rumbling, but it would have to wait until tomorrow when he sold his containers or got his money from Johnte or Timo.

He was almost nodding off to sleep when someone blocked his light. It was Malkia in her high heels and miniskirt. She had a cut on her cheek and her arm, and her left eye had big dark bruises. In her hands was a paper bag that smelled like a meal. Kesho looked at her with warm eyes and smiled for the first time that day.